Whisper Hollow

BELIEVE

BY L.L. MACY

Happy Reading Cassy !!

Lorna Macy
4-20-13

Strategic Book Publishing and Rights Co.

Strategic Book Publishing and Rights Co.
12620 FM 1960, Suite A4-507
Houston, TX 77065
www.sbpra.com

ISBN: 978-1-60976-629-0

*Dedicated to the knowledge, power
and release only reading can produce.*

Around the world and throughout time
One word
Has been spoken
Between father and son;
Mother and daughter;
Friend to friend; and
Even enemy to enemy.
In any language, it gives
Strength and willpower; and
Determination and fortitude.
In Finland they say, "Uskoa",
In Germany, "Glauben";
Spain, "Creer";
Romania, "Crede"; Italy, "Credere";
China, "xiang1 xin4;
…And in English we say
Believe!

Many, many books exist in the world today, powerful books, all of them.

You smirk. Do you not believe? Does not a book inspire feelings of sadness, yet happiness as well? Can it not show you terrible evil, yet great love; or open your eyes to wonders you thought never were? Most of all; can it not take you on a journey into imagination that seems so real that reality ceases to exist? ...Or is reality merely an extension of our own imagination.

Once, before there were fables or any stories of old, there was the adventure from which all adventures come...from a time long ago, when they were first created. Once, one book was created and left unwritten. Believed to possess greater powers than words alone, it was passed down through the ages, inspiring yet twelve more. All were stored in a wooden box dubbed the Trunk of Life... guarded by good, desired by evil. Once, all people and faeries alike believed in the power of those books and the need to preserve them for the future so that they may inspire others. Once, one man stood against seven strikes of evil for just that reason, because he believed...believed that anything was possible between the covers of a book.

CHAPTER I

Once...

A HUGE brown and gold hawk lifted his wings in unison but one time, gliding effortlessly over the forest below, wings outstretched. His large hooded eyes scanned the peaks of the mountains surrounding the small valley that gave little protection against the strong northern wind cascading over them; and it was getting stronger yet, even for him. Churning, boiling black clouds began to rise behind those peaks and he watched as the fog crept its way up and over the highest of them, down towards the valley and forest below.

He was Cedrick, the eyes and ears and sometimes even the very thoughts of his master, Ciera, Queen of the Faeries. Searching the dead forest he spotted Enol, the knight would be magician; then shifted his eyes to the north once more focusing on the fog snaking its way through downed trees and brown grass; pushed along by the power of the black clouds above it and the evil within.

Cedrick thought of this once beautiful forest. The majestic

oaks and aspens, grassy meadows and widespread wildflowers were all just a memory now…yet another price paid for control of the Trunk of Life. Again he searched for the knight, finding him once more, kneeling, holding in his right hand what the great bird knew could only be the Sword of Ciera, the last of his seven keys. Cedrick took a deep breath, hoping the faith and belief his queen had placed in this young knight would be magician, was not in vain. He waited, soaring high above, wings still outstretched, knowing that if Enol failed, he must take action. At all cost the Trunk of Life must be saved.

His eyes narrowed and he turned his attention back to the fog. It was everywhere slinking, slithering like a snake, creeping, winding and curling 'round the withered trunks of once great trees, but this was not just any fog; it was searching… searching for the knight would be magician and the knight would be magician was waiting for it. Enol stood, feet planted in the gray dust that now coated the ground, his back against the trunk of a huge oak that had been snapped nearly in half. He knew that it was coming, the last effort from an almost defeated enemy. The last fight he must face for control of the Trunk of Life.

The northern wind slapped his face, twisting and blowing his hair up and around. Twigs and leaves swirled around, glancing off him. He turned making sure the Trunk of Life was still at his feet, as his mind's eye ran through the memories of the last six keys and evils' attempt to gain control of the books. The wolf, the Cane of Narzio, the braided rope, the mirror, the cask of water and the lamp, all had helped him in great ways, saving his life many times over. All had helped get him here to this forest with the last of the seven keys…the Sword of Ciera, Queen of the faeries herself. He could just see the poisonous fog now. Soon it would sense the life within him, attack and attempt to consume the Trunk of Life. The knight would be magician pulled the Queen's sword from its sheath and knelt, drawing in a deep breath, the sword now feeling heavier than it ever had. The battle for the trunk had been a long one and every muscle in his body screamed in pain as he lifted the sword slowly and spoke to the stone it held.

"Sword of Ciera, you are the last of the seven keys. Please, help me now. The Trunk of Life is almost safe. With your help, it will be for a very long time, I promise this now." His head jerked up, a woman's voice; it was everywhere and nowhere at the same time, seeming to float on the very air around him.

"Raise your sword, knight! Face the stone away from you and say my name!" it said. Enol lifted the sword, turning the hilt of the sword containing the stone away from him as he had been directed and as the fog began to engulf him, he raised it high saying, "Ciera!" Light shot forth from the stone instantly, placing itself between the knight would be magician, the Trunk of Life and the deadly fog. Enol watched as trees started bending back and forth again and again. He felt his hair stop moving and the absence of wind upon his face. He watched as the leaves and loose twigs swirled, still circling around him in the wind yet never touching him.

"The wind is blowing but I feel nothing!" he thought aloud. He watched in amazement, still holding the sword high in the air, suddenly feeling wind at his back. A strong and whipping southern wind was pushing the fog away…that was when he saw them. Two angered faces etched on a mixture of fog and dark clouds as they were forced to retreat and then were gone.

Everything stopped as the light slowly faded from the sword. The knight would be magician lowered it, sliding it back into the sheath that was tied to his waist. He watched in awe as the rest of the dark clouds seem to melt away; and blue sky could once again be seen over what was left of the forest. The seventh key had served him well, protecting him from almost certain death. He would return it to its owner…a woman he had met only in a dream. His eyes settled on the Trunk of Life as he drew in a deep breath. Thoughts of all that had happened raced in his mind as the forest around him fell silent. "Enol." His eyes snapped up searching the trees around him. "Enol, it is I, Ciera."

A broken tree to the right of him seemed to move. Wooden arms, legs, clothing, and a face appeared and the Queen of the Faeries herself stepped into full view. The boots she wore stopped just above her knees; the wrap around her shoulders barely brushing the top of them. She was tall and lean, her wings full and tapered, an empty sheath hung across her back stretching down to the back of her thigh. The crown on her head was a band of gold with four points, each with a different jewel beset in it. Hair flowed out and away from her face on an invisible wind and she was smiling. Enol smiled back.

He knew little of her, only the legends. She was Queen over all faeries, the keeper in the balance of good and evil. The knight would be magician bent down on one knee realizing as he did that she…she was the woman from his dream. He lowered his eyes without wanting to, such beauty.

"Please," Ciera said softly, "Rise. You have fully earned my respect and that of the faerie kingdom. Enol, you have saved the Trunk of Life." With that her delicate wings folded back into a sort of cape under the empty sheath on her back and she now bowed her own head toward the knight would be magician.

"My lady," he said gently taking her hand, bringing them face to face. He could see the strength she possessed in the way she held his stare. "When you came to me in my dream you said that you believed in me and my destiny to save the Trunk of Life. Believe me now that I will honor and keep the promise I have made."

Ciera looked deep into the knight would be magician's eyes seeing the courage and wisdom she knew he already possessed. "My father knew of you many years ago. He had a vision; a vision that a man named Enol would eventually control the Trunk of Life. That a knight would be magician would survive seven strikes of evil," she paused shifting her stare from his eyes, not wanting to though, and looked around at the dead forest, continuing. "And as for your promise…" Her left eyebrow rose and she looked once more in his eyes, "I would like to help you keep it!"

The faerie queen stepped backwards, twirling in a slow deliberate circle; all the while moving her hands in the air as if she were painting. As she turned the whole forest changed, grass grew, poking up through the strewn twigs and leaves. Flowers spread everywhere, and the withered trunks of once great trees were healed as they grew new branches laden with fresh leaves. Now the ground shook beneath Enol's feet; and he turned to see a tiny sprout push through the dirt and become a sapling, then a young tree…then a mighty oak. He stood back in amazement and turned toward the beautiful faerie, not knowing what to say.

Ciera just smiled and spoke first. "You will need a home and safe place for the Trunk of Life." She turned him gently again toward the tree and standing behind him, brought a flat hand down and past his eyes. Enol's mouth widened speaking a silent 'whoa!'

In the moment it had taken to cover his eyes, she had transformed the mighty oak into a home. A large arched door stood at its base with what seemed to be a smaller door in its top section. He watched in amazement as grooves formed at the bottom of it and moved upward. The door was somehow carving itself! His eyes drifted upward toward the round window that stood open above it, the same thing, it was carving itself.

Enol turned to the beautiful faerie with one eyebrow up and a half smile staring in awe and admiration. "Incredible. Think you can teach me that trick?" Ciera stared back at Enol smiling at his smile with his one eyebrow up. "It is not a trick, it is magic and I am just the deliverer of it as it passes through me from my ancestors."

The knight would be magician knitted his eyebrows, "Tell me more."

Ciera gave him back his half grin with one of her own. "I will tell you this, true magic good or evil never dies. Now come, let me show you your new home."

She reached her hand toward the massive door but paused when Enol's hands touched her shoulders.

"What is…," The knight would be magician stopped short and cocked his face sideways in confusion as the ripples that seemed to swim up the door came to an abrupt halt, forming into what could only be faces. Yes, faces that spoke Ciera's name and quibbled over who would speak first. "Or should I say who?" he continued over the top of them. Ciera answered his question by addressing the two faces by name. "Id, Odd! Shush up for one second." Both faces were immediately quiet, eyes upon their new Queen. She had saved them but weeks before, a story for another time. Ciera continued, "We will talk later this evening, for now, practice your traveling skills as you will be accompanying me when I leave." At that, the faces disappeared back down the trunk of the massive oak and into the ground. Enol watched in amazement as they did but his face showed concern as he looked back up toward her.

"You are leaving?" he said hesitantly.

"One day," she answered back with a wink. "But for now

we have much work to do; and lessons to learn first my knight would be magician." Opening the massive door with a gentle push, she led the way in. Enol picked up the Trunk of Life and followed her through the doorway saying, "Just tell me one thing, whose side are those guys on?" Ciera turned toward him her left eyebrow up and arched. "Ours."

* * *

Ciera stayed at Enol's new home for some time teaching him many things about the books and the magic they held. That he must always believe in their power and that between the covers of a book; all things are possible. The first six keys had returned safely and been absorbed by the books; her sword, the seventh, now filled her once empty sheath and hung on one of the hooks next to the huge arched door. Together they set up the library arranging the first twelve on the shelves; but the thirteenth Ciera left in the trunk. Enol watched as she did this, suddenly placing his hand on hers, the one that held the lid as he glanced to the books on the shelves then back to the book in the trunk.

"Why is this one titled and the others not?" His hand was still on top of hers. He did not wait for an answer. He read the title, "Book of Anisoptera."

Ciera's eyes flashed toward him. "You say the name correctly." Her thoughts reeled. She knew the name of this thirteenth book because her father had told her. The book had never revealed its name on the cover before, not ever…that is, to no one but this knight would be magician.

Enol smiled almost blushing, "Only from a childhood story my mother told me years ago. It means dragonfly."

Ciera smiled at him seeing the faraway look in his eyes and was unable to stop herself from reading his thoughts. He was remembering the story and his mother; and all the while the letters on the book in the half closed trunk glowed without their knowledge. She pulled her eyes from him, lowering them to the top of the trunk, slightly ashamed at having invaded his private thoughts; and placed her other hand on top of his pushing gently on the lid closing it, barely catching a glimpse of the glow as the latch clicked shut. Instantly she reopened it to confirm what she had seen but no glow came from within.

"What's the matter?" asked Enol.

"I thought..." Her voice trailed off as she looked up at him and once again closed it. Turning to face him fully she said, "This book is the thirteenth book. It was created first by the Old Ones, the Mighty Ones who could foresee the future; and the powers one book would need to provide between its covers...magic, yes; but knowledge was the ultimate goal. One book created to inspire all others."

Her hand moved waving toward the other twelve. "The Mighty Ones knew that this book would inspire my Father Quinn to create twelve more as it was passed down from generation to generation to him." She paused now, turning away from him stepping toward the shelves, spinning back toward him again. "They also knew of you Enol and that you would one day find a way to use the twelve to inspire others, books of knowledge, inspiration, happiness and even sadness for the world of the future to come."

The knight would be magician stared at the books on the shelves now, his face serious, eyebrows once more knit in thought. Ciera held back from reading them.

"Are these books connected in some way?" he asked it hesitantly; and she noticed answering simply, "In all ways. Their power is equally shared between them".

His ears heard all that she said; but all the while in his mind he marveled at her beauty watching as she moved towards the trunk, and patted it on the top saying, "This book could rewrite the stories of the other twelve. It could control them, changing our lives forever." She had paused, gazing momentarily out the window, thoughts seemingly far away. "A book I believe, that the very power to keep us safe will run through one day. A book so powerful that if opened by evil, all would be lost; for it is a book, even with all the power it holds; that is, as of yet unwritten…its destiny unknown."

* * *

…And so it was that the thirteenth book stayed locked in the Trunk of Life and was hidden by Ciera's father Quinn while Enol continued his training as a knight magician. They had late dinners and each told of their lives up to this point. Ciera explained her powers and their limitations. How she had to wait till the fog and clouds were virtually upon him before the powers of her ancestors would work through her sword, pushing the wind that had blown them away.

At this point Enol had held up his hand, "So you are saying that up to the seventh key, your sword, I was bait?"

Half smiles had come to both faces, eyebrows arching; and Ciera had answered simply, "Well, yes," adding immediately, "And a very good piece of bait you were, luring and surviving each strike of evil."

They laughed together at this and Enol took her hand into his still smiling at her.

"Next time however, I would like to know when I am going to be the bait, okay?" he said as his other hand traced the outline of her chin.

She smiled back at him answering immediately, "Agreed." Suddenly Enol's smile faded as he stared at her face and hers had followed, "What?" she asked.

He told her of the faces he had seen. They had seemed

etched, features only; but had been able to move independently apart from the fog and clouds on which they seemed to ride. One, he was sure, had been a woman who resembled her. Ciera turned away from him at once her wings flaring and the smile disappearing from her face. She snapped back toward him wings still flared, shoulders square in defiance, "That would have been Anya, evil sister of the Queen of the Faeries herself…yes…me. The other would have been Rhetoric, one time magician apprentice to my father; Rhetoric, who desires the Trunk and the books inside for his own evil agenda; Rhetoric, who would surely kill for the thirteenth."

He touched her face again and she softened her stance, her wings settling. "I can see the resemblance," he said tracing down her cheek again, his eyes softening, "It is said that one must sometimes take the good with the bad."

That was when he first kissed her and she had let him.

The two of them grew close, fell in love and had a child named Madrena. Enol soon became the true magician he was meant to be; and together they named the new land *Whisper Hollow.*

CHAPTER II

Now…

CIERA'S DREAM had been so vivid, her father so alive looking and her heart had swelled, remembering how much she missed him and her mother. If one could cry in a dream, surely, she had. When she finally awoke her face was wet with tears. His appearance had been the same as she had last seen him, the lines of life encircling his eyes, but softening when he smiled and spoke to her.

"My dear daughter, I have missed you."

"And I you my father," she answered.

He hugged her gently and stood back, hands still on her upper arms. "You must return home my dear, evil is trying to open the trunk…the thirteenth book needs you."

Her minds eye briefly envisioned a bright green and she responded, "It is safe, father."

Again the lines of life softened as he smiled once more. "You are correct but once more evil will try to attain it and the other twelve books. This time must be its last. This time you must rid the world of the threat to take the power of books from the future, completely and forever."

In the dream, she stood before him, her sword in its sheath on her back, the dragonfly dagger on her side. His eyes had lowered toward the dagger, and then back into hers. "Keep close guard on that; you will need it."

The dragonfly dagger was almost 14 inches in length. Its sheath, reinforced with the same metal that encased its hilt. A true master had created it. The metal was carved and was deeply intricate and ornate. Three jewels were beset in the handle, one blue, one red and one green. Around them the metal had been shaped into elegant swirls signifying the sky above, the land below and the love that should always be between it. The blade itself was razor sharp. It had never been used. Legend goes that only a dragonfly dagger can pierce the skin of a true magician...good or evil. The knife must be sharp, untainted and unused having never pierced skin of any kind or drawn blood...a virgin blade if you wish. Ciera kept it at her side always as her father had asked. She had been told in the past that a specific use would arise for it, nothing more.

Her fingers had lightly caressed the hilt of it as she watched him reach into the depths of the floor length robe he had worn in the dream. He produced a small scroll.

"Enol has aged, my daughter; you will need this in the new fight against an old enemy."

"What is this?" she asked as she took it from him raising one eyebrow.

"I must go now Ciera; just follow the directions and the map. Be careful, evil has learned many new tricks. Believe!" Lightly, he touched her face and she had felt it. Slowly he had faded away, all the while looking into her eyes.

"Father! I have more questions!" she had yelled in her dream but he had not returned.

She awoke with a tear stained face, wondering what the scroll could have contained. The stream that cut its way down the hillside, where she had made camp the night before called to her in its own babbling way and she rose, washing her face in it, waking up with its coolness, as it cleared her mind. She used the inside of her shawl to wipe off the excess water, and gazed up at the sky above. The sun was just about ready to peak over the mountains to the east; and the clouds seemed to be exclusive to the valleys as they hugged their floor. Turning toward the now out fire she thought of her husband, Enol. If he were here, he would just be finishing his second cup of coffee; she missed him. No one and no dream had to twist her arm to return to Whisper Hollow.

She had only a small pack to carry; and she turned to retrieve it. Not one, but both eyebrows rose when she saw the scroll…the scroll from her dream, and she remembered her grandfather's last words, "Believe!" Slowly she bent toward it, picking it up gently, unrolling it. Her eyes scanned it quickly, a smile coming to her face. There would be a sacrifice on her part but her husband was worth it. Madrena and the books were worth it. Whisper Hollow was worth it.

Quickly she rolled it back up, placing it in her pack, and called for the two faces that traveled with her. A mere moment passed and there they were, side by side on the log, just to the right of the fire pit.

"You called Ciera?" they both chimed together. She peered down at the two faces remembering back when they had first met. Both faces were the last of their kind. They had been gnomes of different tribes, whose fellow tribesman had one by one eliminated the other till there was but one of each. The two of them, Id and Odd, now hung on the log before her.

She had intervened just in the nick of time, stopping Odd's dagger from hitting its mark, disarming them both with a single swing of her sword saying, "I have watched you and yours for years, slaughtering each other for simply the differences you both hold sacred; the very differences that make us all unique. No more."

The two gnomes had stared at her with hatred, then back at each other with even more.

Odd had been first to speak. "You have no right to tell us what we can and cannot do," he had snarled, with Id adding, "My people have only defended themselves," his eyes shot towards Odd, "They started this fight."

She replied simply, raising her sword once more high on her right side, "I am Ciera, Queen of the Faeries, and I have every right. It takes two to keep fighting, and because of your unwillingness to resolve this petty fight based on indifference, you will now serve me until I feel you have proven yourselves and your prejudice thoughts have ceased."

With that she swung the sword, passing it just above their heads striking the tree at their back. "I banish you to the wood never to touch the soil or water that surrounds us; never to walk among the rest of the world upright. You will serve me and fight others like yourselves." As her sword hit the tree, they were sucked into the crevice it created, only the outlines of their faces showing in the wood.

Acceptance of their fate had come slowly, but they had adjusted nicely, proving themselves repeatedly throughout the years. She knelt down tickling Odd's chin then passed her hand gently across Id's brow. "Seems we must return home my friends, any objections?"

The two faces smiled broadly. "None here!" said Id automatically with Odd adding, "I'll second that!"

Their queen smiled back at them reading their almost identical thoughts. "Where would we be, if you had not stopped us so many years ago? Dead, most probably."

She had shown them the value of enjoying the differences between the assorted cultures they had experienced in the many years in which they had served her. Life was an adventure now, not a struggle. Life was good.

Ciera responded, "You have both proven yourselves many times over. I am so very proud of you, and how far you have progressed. I could release you from the wood that imprisons you today, if you so desire, but I must ask you to stay as you are for now. Once more evil comes for the books, and in your present state you could be a great advantage in the fight against it. It is your choice to make."

Id looked over at Odd, then back to his Queen. "I feel I speak for both us when I say our debt to you for what you have done for us is yet unpaid. How can we help?"

Their beautiful queen spread her wings as she strapped her small pack on her back nodding at their choice and smiled, "Just keep up with me for now!"

She flew up just above the treetops, turning towards home, silently sending a message out to Cedrick to meet her there. Id and Odd raced from the log to the trees, jumping from one branch to another, both of them so excited about returning home that they did not notice the blackened figure that lurked at the forest edge, just inside the darkness watching them, and listening…but Ciera did.

She turned her head back toward the dark spot, staring at it, letting it know she saw it then turned her thoughts to home, the scroll and then something else; the glow of the lettering so long ago…the glow of the thirteenth book.

* * *

Enol sat at his massive desk stroking his now gray beard, staring at the books sitting on the shelves with red rimmed eyes. Just one sign, just let me see one sign. Something was up with them;

he knew it…felt it deep down. Then there was the fading. It had happened just out of the corner of his eye. You know the place where you wonder if you really did see it, but he was sure he had. It had been the book of Fire and Smoke that had faded, becoming sort of transparent and then it was back. It had glowed, its power seeming to radiate from it as if the book itself was fighting some unseen battle, struggling to remain in its place on the shelf.

He took a long deep breath knowing deep down that who-ever was trying to possess the books would get it right sooner or later and the books would start disappearing. He was older now. Would he be able to fight as he had before? Fight for control of the books, and win once more.

His thoughts now turned to Ciera who had been gone so long, too long. Not only did he want to talk with her about the books; he just wanted his wife home. Her duties as Queen were many though, and he respected her for fully living up to her legacy as the balance of good and evil.

Enol's eyes never left the books as his thoughts of Ciera continued. His beautiful wife had long ago taught him of the powers the books held, and how her father had intended to use the books when first created. However, with the continual threat of evil's attempt to possess the books, Quinn had had no choice but to lock them away in the *Trunk of Life*, hidden, until a certain young knight would be magician from his vision would come along to protect them, that is.

Enol smiled his half smile remembering how Quinn had introduced himself just after watching him joust…and lose. He had come straight into the arena, looked straight down at his face as he sat up from the fall from his horse, and said, "No future son in law of mine loses! Get up and try again." Of course Enol had no idea at that time of who Quinn was or what he was talking about. In fact, being a little dazed, he half thought he had dreamed the whole thing until seeing him later in the courtyard to discuss a certain set of books and the future.

Then, once he and Ciera had saved the Trunk of Life, she had shown him the powers between their covers. How each book had the abilities to do whatever was needed to help the reader in their quest, no matter what the quest, hence inspiring books of the future.

He remembered the lines of faeries that had asked to be attached to the books, to be their guardians, and how hard it had been to decide on which ones. …Oh, and then the adventures there had been!

His eyes narrowed, still staring at the shelves of books as he thought of the fading once more. "Only a true magician could be attempting to take these books. The magic they contain holds them on the very shelf they sit, unable to be removed unless called by someone in need. Somehow, they are being fooled." He sat staring at the books, drumming his fingers on his massive desk; wondering who the magician might be, as thoughts of Ciera started filling his head once more. "I need some air," he said aloud as he rose and walked to window.

* * *

Madrena, daughter of Ciera and Enol, stepped lightly down a thin path of clover that wandered throughout Whisper Hollow. She had grown tall and thin like her parents over the years, her beauty upholding her title of Faerie Princess. The wrap that draped her shoulders hung to the back of soft leather boots tied just above her knees with a strand of leather, her purple red hair, braided, hanging down almost as far.

She turned her face upward, half thinking of her mother; half thinking of those lavender blue skies visible just above the treetops, and that they looked particularly bright today. Her fingers played gently with the emerald necklace around her neck, a present from her mother at birth; and she looked down at the clover still underfoot, smiling. As a child, Madrena had discovered that no matter what direction in Whisper Hollow she went the clover spread out in front of her, its path always leading her home…in fact, right to her front door! It had been something her mother, Ciera; had come up with. She told her, "You will always be safe here sweetie; you will never be lost as the clover will show you the way. It will always know where to take you." Madrena squinted down at the clover wondering how her mother had accomplished it, and about the magic she had used to do it.

Today, it led her to the outcropping that overlooked the land beyond Whisper Hollow. This was her favorite place, a place where she could think and imagine. Clouds floating above could become dragons with magnificent wings, their pointed faces topped with huge plumage almost as big as their bodies. Madrena sat with one leg dangling over the side, waving at the valley below as she moved it back and forth. She fanned her wings, soaking up the late afternoon sun as the small rising breeze moved up through them, and tousled the loose strands of her hair.

She thought of her mother and threw hands in the air showing her youth, flipping her eyes upward, wanting to scream, "I want my Mom!" out loud, but she didn't. She was very proud of her Mom and knew deep down she was where she needed to be, and would be here if she could, but when? She really did miss her. Maybe Dad knows when she'll be home. Madrena stood and took one last look at the world beyond and turned, following the clover once more and headed the short distance home.

* * *

The great hawk could just see the top branches of the mighty oak; home to his now good friend, Enol, his Queen and their daughter Madrena. He glided silently, lifting his wings just once to sustain the speed he had already attained. His queen had called him, and he had wasted no time in answering. Cedrick thought of the things Ciera had told him...about the good things Enol had accomplished with the books. How he attached faeries to them, allowing the books to use the incredible powers they held to help people in need; while inspiring those same people to write books of their adventures and their lessons learned which inspired even more to believe in the power of books and the power between their covers. "Brilliant!" he thought. His knight would be magician had become a true magician indeed!

Cedrick circled, watching Madrena as she walked upon the clover. What a beautiful young woman she had become. He then turned once more to the oak, thinking of the books, they were getting stronger. He felt it, Ciera felt it, and he was most certain his friend Enol would say he felt it too. Descending, Cedrick rounded the tree toward the open window he knew would be there; spotting Enol just as he poked his head out and looked up at him with that half grin.

"He always knows," thought Cedrick, "oh, if birds could smile..."

Enol pulled in from the window and Cedrick landed on the sill, his eyes immediately on the books. "Good day, my friend," he said to the great hawk, glancing toward the books on the shelf and adding. "You feel it too?"

The big bird bowed and nodded profusely letting out a screech of agreement.

Suddenly, the door burst open and in came Madrena, mouth moving, "Hey Dad! When's Mom coming...Oh! Ceddie! Hi! It has been so long!" She walked quickly over to the open window stroking the big birds' neck and back. "I am so happy to see you! Surely you must know when my Mom will be here?"

Before the hawk could answer two sets of familiar ripples zoomed up the oak wall, the top ones stopping so quickly that the bottom ones collided with them and the voice of Id could be heard saying, "Ow!" with Odd responding; "Well, stop following so close! You know the rules. Ten inches…ten inches!"

Id answered smugly, "Yeah, yeah."

Madrena started giggling. "Looks like you guys are finally learning to compromise!" "And what did it take," added Enol, "Twenty years?"

Cedrick bobbed his head in agreement as both faces looked at the three of them, poking out rippled wooden tongues. All laughed together and when things quieted, Enol looked from Cedrick to Id and Odd.

"She sent you all," he said simply.

The great hawk screeched once more and the faces responded for him. "Yes." they said in unison. "Our queen sends a message that the trunk is in danger."

Enol turned to his daughter and saw the questioning look form on her face. He placed his hands on her shoulders, squeezing them gently. "Madrena, it looks like you will be seeing your mother very soon!" He hugged her, his eyes on the books at her back, adding, "Tonight is a story night, my dear; please call the faeries."

She pulled back from him, her hands still on his shoulders, asking, "All of them?"

"Yes, all of them." He hesitated very briefly and added, "The soldier faeries as well." Enol did not wait for another response but turned to Id, Odd and Cedrick, "Come let us light a fire, my friends; the shades of darkness are falling fast, and talk."

Madrena watched as her father, the faces and the great hawk went through the door. Something was up. He had been staring at the books, thinking deeply for almost two days now. "What story would father be telling tonight; and what did her mother's message mean?" she wondered as her eyes closed and she summoned all the faeries of Whisper Hollow to story night.

* * *

The dragonfly sat quietly on a leaf, on the branch closest to the talking faces and listened. He was larger than most dragonflies but the green and gold tones in his wings blended with the tree itself. No one noticed him as the one they called Cedrick, stroked the window sill with mighty claws, screeching in a smooth shrill way, as only a hawk can do, saying his hello. His eyes never wavered from Cedrick until the girl with the purple red hair walked over by the great bird, and into view.

"She must be the one," he thought, eyes squinting. His filigree curled up close to his body, his wings took a backward slant. He barely noticed when Enol, Cedrick, and the faces came through the door. He could not take his eyes off of the girl they called Madrena.

* * *

Leaves swayed and crunched ever so quietly, as the faeries of Whisper Hollow flew and hurried into the meeting place. It sat just outside of Enol's home, which let Madrena watch out the window as she kept checking the books for him. Not too often was her father able to sit and tell them the stories of far away lands, or unbelievable stories of magicians past. However, this was no story of yesteryear they had been told…it was one of what was to come.

The night sky was clear and the light from the fire bounced

from face to face as they arrived. All twenty eight of the faeries attached to the books were there, including Sneakin and Peakin; who came fully geared up, both carrying their swords on their backs, complete with the two crescent shaped daggers that fit snugly in the same sheath…warrior faeries, they were always ready for anything. Night and Day, Cinq, Saynk, Sunck and Piggett, Skinnie, and Hyde along with Fire and Smoke had already sat down and of course Id, Odd and Cedrick were there. The soldier faeries were just arriving. They were five in number. Their captain, Emmit was in the lead as they found places among the others.

"Hellos, and "Have not seen you in a whiles," were said quickly as their knight magician raised his hand, asking for silence.

"Please," asked Enol. His voice was calm and even as he looked over at Emmit who still stood. "Please, let us all sit, relax and let the fire warm us, for tonight you will hear a story of the future predicted, a story you will live." The faeries glanced at each other, unsure of how to react to this, unsure of what their knight magician meant. Their eyes returned to him and they listened as he continued. "Tonight, I will tell you the story of a book of books; one that could write your stories, command your books and change your lives forever. A book which Ciera, your queen, and I both believe could channel the very power to keep us safe. A book so powerful that if opened by evil all would be lost, a book that is as of yet unwritten… it's name, The Book of Anisoptera."

There was much whispering amongst the faeries now as Enol paused.

Piggett spoke up, "Is the Book of Anisoptera in danger? Is it missing?"

Before Enol could answer more questions were asked. "Who watches over this book?" "We thought there were only twelve?"

"Has it been here all along in Whisper Hollow?" "Would the book make us evil?"

So many questions were being asked at the same time, Enol held up his hand once more for silence. "I will answer Piggett's questions first. I believe it is, and it may be missing." There was more whispering amongst the faeries.

Enol once again held up his hand. "The Book of Anisoptera or Dragonfly came well before my time and even before Ciera's. It was passed down to her father from his ancestors along with the power within it. It is the Thirteenth Book of your twelve, created first always meant to be opened last. I know not where it is kept only that it exists."

It was Day this time who spoke up first with a grin on her face, she and her brother were the smallest faeries in Whisper Hollow. "Then how do we know it might be missing?" Everyone chuckled.

"A very good question, Day," replied Enol smiling back at her, knowing her playful way.

Sneakin broke in, his right wing snapping, "Have you ever seen this book, Enol?"

The keeper of their books' smile faded, his eyebrows knitted, "I saw this thirteenth book for but an instance many years ago when your Queen and I first placed the other twelve, your books that is, on the shelf. It was hidden by Quinn himself. It does indeed exist." He winked at Day, "But somehow I believe not knowing more about it has kept us safe…kept it safe."

More whispering could be heard as Enol paused, looking at the eager faces around him that waited almost breathlessly to know more about this book, the Book of Anisoptera. He wondered. Would this small troop of faeries be enough to save the essence of what was Whisper Hollow? …To defeat the evil now coming for the books? I must have faith in them, he thought. In all their many adventures they had never once failed him, or the adult or child they were helping. Id and Odd had brought news that Ciera would arrive early tomorrow, and that it would be necessary to bring the faeries up to date on what was to come, that once again evil was trying to get to the books.

Enol leaned his head back seeing Madrena in the window and gave her a wink, thinking. "Listen carefully, my dear; for all of your magical abilities will be needed, even ones you do not know you possess." She leaned her head to the right, raising an eyebrow, staring back at her father, hearing his thoughts, not noticing the dragonfly who still sat in the tree nearby; her emerald necklace sparkling in the moonlight as her purple red hair splashed around her shoulders. Something inside of her stirred in incredible anticipation, and she winked back at him, a smile creeping to her lips.

...And so Enol told the story of evil's last attempt to control the books. The story he must tell to prepare them for what was to come, to prepare them for tomorrow, and the adventure that lay ahead of them all...

CHAPTER III

More Developments

IT HAD been a long night. He had slept well for the first few hours and then Enol had been awake staring at the books, feet on the desk, arms folded, his thoughts flying everywhere about anything, anywhere and anyone, dozing only twice. His eyes squinted remembering what Cedrick had said about finding the keys…mmm…maybe Madrena could find them. Maybe she could sense which of the books contained them and then a second thought. Would they even need them?

He looked up at the clock on the wall above the books. It was past seven, she should be awake. Removing his feet from the desk, Enol pushed himself to a standing position, stretching. He felt pretty good today despite the lack of sleep. His eyes turned toward the books briefly, counting twelve, paying close attention to the book of Fire and Smoke and he went to wake his daughter.

In his younger days he would have taken the stairs to Madrena's room, two at a time. Not so in the past few years, age was creeping up on him, but somehow, today he felt as if he could and to his surprise he did. At the top of the stairs he turned looking back at them, thinking, "Maybe I'm not too old after all!" He tapped lightly on his daughters' door and waited for an answer.

"Come in!" came the voice on the other side of the door. Enol swung open the door wide, smiling; he knew that voice, and it was not his daughter's!

"Hey beautiful!" Ciera had no chance to return the greeting, as her husband was upon her instantly, kissing her.

She kissed him back then replied, "Hey, handsome!" and snuggled a little deeper into his arms.

Enol leaned back, arms still around his wife's waist, "I am so happy to see you."

"And me you, my husband," replied Ciera, pausing, adding, "Madrena is not here."

Enol never broke her stare, his eyes growing serious. "She is probably just taking an early morning walk."

"No, dear, she is not here. I mean she is not in Whisper Hollow." Ciera saw the sudden panic and concern in his eyes, feeling his arms tense around her; and quickly added, "It is okay though. I felt the same concern at first, but I sense she is fine. So much that, I am sure it is so. I have tried to envision her but only blackness comes through. I will try again later."

Enol's panic drained somewhat away but the concern did not. "But where did she go and why did she not tell us she was leaving? Why did she not leave a note? What if, she could not? She has never been out of Whisper Hollow alone."

Ciera placed a finger gently upon his lips "Maybe there was no time, maybe she was unable to. Maybe she did not *know* she was going. Maybe, just maybe evil has her but I think not, at least not yet. She will be fine, Enol. I cannot explain why I feel she is or will be, I just do. We knew this day would come.

She is not a little girl anymore." Ciera paused, stroking her fingers through his beard. "Our Madrena has grownup, my husband. As my powers have faded, hers are almost at their peak, even if she does not know it yet."

Enol stood back now, taking a good look at his wife. She wore a tunic, soft forest green in color that accented her eyes. The wide brown leather belt around her waist held the Dragonfly Dagger; her father's, the Sword of Ciera hung on her back, safe in its sheath. The top portion of her hair had been braided on the sides, ends tied with more brown leather but the bottom was free and floated on an invisible wind. The wrap she wore hung down past the tops of her boots that ended just above her knees.

He was so in love with her and was just about to tell her so, when out of the corner of his eye he saw the wrap move on its own. Yes, he was sure of it! By itself, it had moved! Ciera saw the questioning look as his eyes followed the moving shapes under her wrap and smiled. "Nip, Tuck…come on out and say hello."

With that, one furry tiny head stuck out next to her neck, and a second furry body scurried out and sat on the handle of the Dragonfly Dagger.

"Honey, meet Nip," Ciera pointed at her neck. "Now Nip can be a little testy at times." The auburn, brown and tan colored ground squirrel stood up on its hind legs, chattering a quick protest. His queen smiled down at him, saying, "He says, only when necessary!"

Enol chuckled.

"And this," continued Ciera, "Is Tuck." Tuck was solid black with just one small smudge of white on his left ear, visible only because he turned to look up at Ciera from the dagger yawning. "He's a big sleeper." She petted them both. "They've been very helpful at times."

Enol looked from Nip to Tuck and could almost say he saw them smile briefly at the compliment from their Queen. He raised his eyebrow as he looked up at her then back down at them again; and Ciera smiled that half smile when she saw it saying, "Have you looked in the mirror yet, my love?"

"Why, do I have sleep in my eyes? A drool mark on my chin?" he replied laughing.

"No my dear, not at all…look." his wife answered, still smiling, now pointing at Madrena's mirror. Enol turned and walked toward the mirror, his eyes never leaving it; his mouth opening in awe as he got closer…was that really him?

He was at least ten years younger in appearance. The lines around his eyes were softened, his hair now brown with just a few gray hairs at his temples.

"But how?" he managed to get out.

"I gave you part of my life," Ciera said simply.

Walking over, she stood beside him before the mirror, changing the subject somewhat. "It is Rhetoric who wants Madrena, and may already have her, my husband. Once more he is after the books. By taking her, he knows you will follow and his chance of killing you and draining your magic from the books is increased. We and all who accompany us to defeat him will be tested. You will need all your strength and then some."

Enol looked at her through the mirror pointing at his younger self. "But how?" he asked again.

Ciera smiled once more at her husband. "From this point on we will be together, our years of life remaining, equal. The how, for now is not important." She turned, facing him, kissing him long and hard adding, "We must gather the faeries of Whisper Hollow now, we must prepare. Reaching our daughter, I fear, will not be easy." Enol nodded in agreement, once again thinking of Madrena. Ciera read his thoughts, touching his face softly. She was not ashamed of doing it anymore; and he had once stated, he wished he could read hers. "Our daughter will be fine; she is smart like her father."

"And her mother," Enol added. He kissed her once more. "I am so glad you are here." "I am too, my love."

Together they called the Faeries of Whisper Hollow and told them of Madrena, her disappearance and the need to prepare. Their Queen explained to them the hard journey ahead and that time was most definitely of the essence. Many of them had wanted to ask questions, but Ciera had held up her hand saying that their questions would be answered once they were on their way. Sneakin had snapped his wings at this, not in anger but in concern for Madrena. "I speak for everyone here," he had said, "That what ever it takes we are all behind you, Enol and Ciera."

Their Queen replied simply, "And it will take my dear Sneakin; for where we must travel to rescue Madrena may even cost you your life!"

All were silent for a moment until Piggett, one of the woodland faeries, asked the question all were wondering. "And the thirteenth book my Queen, is it safe?"

Ciera looked around the group of faeries, then to Enol, then back at Piggett, "That question will be answered soon. Do not worry however, I feel it is."

With that the Faeries of Whisper Hollow had bowed and left to prepare, with no question of their mission. Their only thought now; that their wonderful Madrena was worth their very lives, oh; and possibly how happy Enol looked. So much that he almost looked younger, yes younger but then again, he was always better when their queen was home.

* * *

Ciera stood before her husband; his eyes staring past her in the direction the faeries had flown. "What is it, Enol?"

she asked.

His eyes moved to hers and he answered. "I was remembering the person behind the name. It has been years, many years since the likes of him, thank goodness." He watched as his wife turned to stare out the same window in silence, then turn back toward him.

"Yes, Rhetoric," she started. "My father used to say he was his inspiration yet his opposite."

"How is it that your father came to trust him?" asked Enol.

Ciera's half smile barely graced her face as she looked up at him and said, "Good cannot exist without evil, my love. My father became infatuated with him and the way in which his mind worked. He did not see Rhetoric's plotting or my sisters' for that matter, and their attempts to control the books until it was almost too late."

Enol turned and walked across the library, stopping momentarily to tap his fingers on his desk. "Two days before your father faded away you were called to his room. He spoke to you alone. What was it he said?"

The half smile came fully to her face now. "You are very wise my husband that you ask such a question. A riddle, it was a riddle. One I have always believed was meant not for us but for Madrena...I had almost forgotten."

"Tell me," he said simply.

Ciera pursed her lips briefly. "I cannot, for the answer to it would reveal the location of the thirteenth book and Rhetoric could use that information to not only prevent us from finding our daughter but against Madrena herself."

His eyes met hers. "Then we agree Rhetoric is who we should concentrate on."

"Oh yes," she responded quickly adding, "Absolutely." Ciera walked over to her pack pulling the scroll from it, her smile curled saying, "The how is now important," as she said handed it over to him.

Enol unrolled it asking, "Where did you get this?" as his eyes quickly scanned the contents.

Ciera waited till he was finished reading. "My father came to me two nights ago, he handed this scroll to me in a dream." She paused, thinking; then added, "It was on my pack when I awoke. Somehow it came through the dream with me."

Her husband rolled his lips, saying nothing as he finished looking over the map at the bottom. "This could be a trap my dear, your father is gone. Only one magician other than he could possibly accomplish that." He pulled her close to him, seeing the hurt she still felt at losing her father. "We will proceed with caution. We will believe."

It was at that moment a screech from above their home announced the arrival of their friend Cedrick, causing them both to look toward the open window he always came through. Enol turned and placed his hands on Ciera's shoulders. "I know that you will tell me this riddle in time but how can we get it to Madrena?"

"I believe, my husband; that part of your answer will land in a moment."

Both turned once again to the open window as Cedrick landed quietly on the sill chirping a short hello.

Enol's eyes narrowed and his half smile appeared, "and the other part?"

"That you will have to help me with; I have an idea." Ciera smiled back at him, then nodded a hello at Cedrick and turned walking toward the shelves on which the books sat, running her finger along them.

Enol raised his left eyebrow. "What are you thinking Ciera, I know that look!" He gave her that half smile that makes her weak; and she smiled, raising her own brow now. Cedrick chirped as if seconding Enol's question. The Faerie Queen did not turn, her finger continuing to follow the shelf line until it reached its destination.

"Let's see just how powerful one of your books really is." She paused ever so briefly still looking down at the book. "Have you ever opened one of the books, dear? You, yourself; I mean," Ciera said in her whispery voice, head slightly tilted, the voice Enol knew was used when she had something up her sleeve. He did the half smile thing again, she noticed and continued, "Correct me if I am wrong, but does not the legend of the Trunk state that the book must be opened by the person who will help or needs the help, and the faeries attached to it in order for its magic to be available?" Cedrick chirped again and Enol said nothing, his grin getting bigger yet.

Ciera looked down at the book in front of her tracing the names with the same finger she had traced the shelves with. Then with a single action and to Enol's surprise she lifted the book from its place on the shelf, and turned setting it down on the massive desk, saying, "Should we call for Night and Day?"

Enol winked at his wife. "Not necessary, the book itself has already done that!" "Really…" she answered barely finishing the word as the smallest two faeries of Whisper Hollow flew through the window. They had been cleaning and readying their weapons when they got the calling and had come at once fully geared up.

"Thank you both for coming so quickly," started Ciera, thinking to herself, "These books are incredible!"; and receiving Enol's quiet thank you back instantly, causing her to smile but shoot him a questioning look. The two small faeries stood on Enol's desk both staring down at their book, both knowing well the rules of it.

Night was first to speak as he pointed towards it. "How is

this possible?"

Their queen answered quickly, eyes sparkling, "There will be no traveling involved on this mission for the ones who are in need stand before you, and the ones who will help are here too." She nodded toward Cedrick.

"Wow!" exclaimed Night instantly as Day echoed, "Ditto."

Enol chuckled from behind his wife causing her to turn and smile at him. "Yes, she's pretty amazing!" he said as their eyes met. Cedrick squawked in agreement, oh if birds could smile he thought.

Ciera turned to him whispering, "Oh, but you do!" lightly tickling him on the neck. She turned back towards the desk. "Once again please correct me if I am wrong, but in one of your recent adventures you dove into your book, into the World of Dreams to rescue a young boy."

Night nodded as Day said, "We had no idea our book had such power!"

Their Queen listened, her eyes shining with excitement as the two small faeries glanced down at their book once more on the desk. "In doing so you brought back the Cane of Narzio, did you not?"

Night spoke up this time. "Yes, my Queen. You could sort of say the cane brought us back into the real world; as if, it knew 'it' and 'we' did not belong there in the World of Dreams…as if it had been waiting for us to need 'it'."

"It did know, and it had been waiting," their queen answered. "You see the Cane of Narzio was created for the son of a distant cousin of mine who was born with just one leg. It was powerful enough to do whatever was needed of it, to take him wherever he needed to go. As with your books it had a sense, a sense of knowing when it was needed; and as with most magical items created long ago it was desired by evil and finally stolen." Ciera paused briefly, light from the nearby fire dancing in her eyes. "But the thief would be sadly disappointed as this cane could only be used by good alone, and this must be where your young friend came in. King Darien of the World of Dreams is indeed an evil man. He needed someone good to wield the cane and to control its power. I, myself, had all but forgotten about it until Enol told me of your adventure." Ciera then turned to her husband, "Do you still have the cane?"

"Yes, my love." he answered smiling.

She marveled at its simplicity when he returned and handed it to her. It resembled a mere stick, wooden, with a section of vine that started at the bottom and wound around it ending just below the hilt shaped hand rest. Real leaves sprouted from the practically dead looking vine, showing life still existed within.

Ciera lifted her eyes slowly; a familiar raised eyebrow graced her face as she handed the cane to Night and stroked the neck of Cedrick. "You will need this to find your way once more." She paused for a reaction and receiving none continued as she walked around the desk and opened a drawer pulling out pen and paper. "Night, you and Cedrick will fly into the book." She paused and turned to Day, "You, my dear, will be needed to help pull them, if necessary, from the book like it was in your last adventure." Her face grew serious now. "As with the World of Dreams, the book can get you in the right area but not necessarily right to Madrena. You may have to look for her. Cedrick will not only help with the search but will aide in hiding you Night. Your dark color should blend well with his and four eyes are better than two. Where you are going could be very dangerous for a faerie of Whisper Hollow to be all alone in, so stay together. If Madrena has been taken by evil, I can only imagine the surroundings."

Ciera, now sitting behind the massive desk, bowed her head toward the paper and pen in her hand. A single tear hit the paper, and Enol rushed behind her kissing the back of her neck. She looked up momentarily reassuring him that all was okay, placing her hand on his; and said, "My dear, Night will need a sheath to hold the cane safe until it is needed to get back home. Will you get that for him?"

He squeezed her shoulder and was walking toward the closet when Day spoke up. "My brother can use my sheath." With that she removed her dagger and hung the sheath around his neck and back; slicing off the bottom of it quickly, without hesitation, with the blade of her own dagger to accommodate the Cane of Narzio.

Night and Day's eyes met and he said, "Thanks Sis!"

"No problem bro," she answered with a wink.

Ciera finished the short note to their daughter, carefully folding the paper as she stood and attached it to Cedrick's leg with a single strand of leather. "No one must read this except Madrena, no one. Once read it must be destroyed for her safety."

"It will be so, my Queen," replied Night simply.

"One more thing," responded Ciera. "The rules, set in place by my ancestors, govern our magic even today. They allow us only seven keys to defeat evil, or seven aides of magic. The Cane of Narzio will be considered one of them. Madrena must read the note. You must succeed. The use of one key must not be wasted as we do not know how many keys will be needed or we will even be allowed."

"Excuse me," spoke up Day, "I'm confused. How come they can not just bring Madrena home to us when they find her?"

"Can we do that if it is possible?" seconded Night.

Enol and Cedrick sat silent. In the years of service to their Queen they knew the answer before it was spoken.

"Once again evil has set in motion its attempt to gain control of the books. Madrena will know from all her teachings she is more valuable to us where she is…on the inside," Ciera answered. She turned towards her husband who stood behind her, the book at her back. His lips were tight, his eyebrows knitted, she placed her hand on his.

"Madrena will be fine. She must and we must believe." The Faerie Queen straightened her back, eyes dancing once more. "Now let's open this book."

"I think it is ready for that," Enol answered quickly, his eyes looking past her as he turned her around to see for herself.

"Does that happen every time, Night and Day?" he added almost stammering.

"Every time," they answered together.

"It's beautiful," uttered Ciera as she recalled the glow in the trunk long ago.

"Yes," they said again in unison.

The pages of the book shone. The white yellow light even made its way through the cover, illuminating the title…*Night & Day*. It was bright but comfortable and inviting. "It's time," spoke up Day.

"Yes," echoed Night nodding toward his Queen. Ciera looked from him to the cover and placed her hands upon the book. It was warm and a humming could just be heard and felt. It wanted them to open it and ever so gently, Ciera did.

The book wasted no time. A picture starting drawing itself on the first page almost immediately as if the book had been waiting breathlessly, and now had been unleashed.

Cedrick, now sitting on Enol shoulder, chirped softly in his ear. "I know my friend. It is truly amazing." Ciera glanced up at her husband and the hawk; a puzzled look crossing her face again for just a moment but she returned her concentration to the book.

"It looks like a door of some kind," she said.

"It is," said Day.

"A trapdoor," added Night, "It knows we have the Cane. Turn the page, my Queen." She did and this time the picture was drawn even faster and the door was halfway open! "One more my Queen," said Night again. This time the picture was already drawn, and light spilled forth from the opening! "There is our invite, Cedrick!" Night said.

The huge hawk squawked as he flew over landing on the desk next to the open book.

"I think he wants you to climb on," said Enol.

"Yes, he does," added Ciera, another questioning curious look showing on her face again as she looked over at her husband. She gave him the half smile then turned her attention back to Ceddie and Night.

"First and foremost, you two be careful; but at all costs you must succeed! Deliver the riddle and get back here you will be needed in the defeat of evil."

Day now stood on the opposite side of the book from her brother and the great hawk. "Night, it may be different this time but remember the World of Dreams? After we had been there almost a full day and night the trapdoor started closing…"

"I remember and we will hurry." He winked at his sister and flew up on Cedrick's wing.

"Godspeed!" said Enol. They flew up and then down into the trapdoor that now filled the entire page, glowing even more brilliantly than before; and disappeared into it.

Ciera stepped back away from the book brushing her husbands arm, and then spoke directly to the smallest faerie of all. "You and your brother are very brave my dear. Guard the book and await their return; then, join up with us in Amberwood as soon as you can."

"Without a doubt," replied the now brightly lit faerie,

adding with confidence, "They will succeed, my Queen."

Ciera nodded at her in admiration noticing how Day held her dagger in the left hand with the right hand ready to grab the Cane of Narzio, as she stared alertly into the trapdoor. "Yes, I have no doubt they will."

Enol slid his hand into his wife's hand and turned her toward him. "Amberwood?"

"We need more help and the faerie warriors that live there will be a great addition; and besides, they will know how to get in touch with the Wind Riders," she answered.

"Wind Riders?" Enol had that, 'who', look on his face.

His wife smiled at him, straightening his collar, "Honey, you have been guarding the books way to long, you need to get out more."

They both chuckled and she tugged gently on his hand leading him toward the door but paused just before it saying, "How did you know that?"

"Know what, my dear."

"What Cedrick wanted Night to do?"

"I'm not sure, kind of just popped in my head. It probably has something to do with that waking up younger thing I read about!" he laughed and winked at her.

Ciera smiled back eyebrow raised, "Excuse me for one minute, my love."

She disappeared up the stairs and was back instantly saying, "It is time to leave I hope the others are ready," as she looked down gently pulling open the door.

"Oh, they are," said Enol catching sight of Sneakin through the window. The Queen of the Faeries looked out to find all the faeries of Whisper Hollow standing and sitting in the clearing outside.

Cinq, one of the water faeries warbled, "My Queen, we are ready to find our Princess."

CHAPTER IV

Madrena and the Riddle

THE OVERSIZED dragonfly sat next to Madrena as she lay on the cavern floor sleeping. His wings spread wide and open, showing their bright forest green and gold tones even in the darkness of the cave. There had been no choice; he had to bring her here, somewhere safe. Rhetoric was close to making his move for her and the books, he was sure of it. As Adren, warrior prince of the Anisoptera order, he was destined to protect her. Groomed by his ancestors for this very moment…as she was by hers. He moved his wings, lightly fanning her face; and she moved, a hint of a smile crossing her face.

"My dear Madrena, you are very beautiful." Again he fanned her and she brought a hand to her face rubbing her eyes. Quietly he moved to the shadows. Their meeting was not yet right.

Eyes still shut Madrena continued rubbing them with one hand, propping her body up sideways with the other. Slowly she opened them blinking back the grogginess she felt, dreaming of breakfast, but it was not her bedroom that met her open eyes. She pushed herself to a sitting position, it was dark but not to dark to see. It was a cave of some sort that was for sure. Empty, except for the random boulders that seemed to have fallen from the roof of the cave. "Great!" came out of her mouth as she looked up seeing yet more that were soon to fall.

Madrena looked over at the wall on her right. Water was running down in a steady trickle, creating a slight puddle on the floor. Something sparkled…green? Her eyes widened. She dove towards it; scooping it up with one hand as the other hand went to her neck. "My necklace!" she whispered aloud, her hand still clasping her throat as she clutched it tightly.

It had never been off, never in all her life. A tear welled up in one eye as she thought of her mother and how she would miss her visit today. It must have fallen off when…. "When what? How did I get here and where is here!" she screamed aloud; but that question would have to be answered later as her necklace suddenly started vibrating to the point of humming in her hand. Madrena looked down in amazement; the emerald was glowing and as it got brighter the hum got louder. Until just as suddenly as the vibrating had started, the emerald popped open revealing an inner chamber and something was inside. She bent her head a little lower to see.

It appeared to be a sort of box, square with a hump on top. She squinted her eyes. It was so small! That was when she noticed the latch on one side.

"Oh my! It's a trunk!" One eyebrow rose as her mothers did and the corner of her mouth curled into a half smile as her fathers did. …And the dragonfly watched from the shadows.

Madrena looked up and around the cave, maybe this was just a dream; maybe she was lying at home in her bed. Maybe her mother would arrive in moments and awaken her, but something inside told her no. This was not a dream. It was then that she heard the familiar screech from outside the cave and the blackness beyond.

"Ceddie?" Standing, she tipped her necklace to the side causing the trunk to fall into her open left hand, and snapped the emerald lid back down with her thumb; dropping it at her feet on the cave floor as Night flew through the cavern entrance with Ceddie close behind. The small dark faerie flew to a rock outcropping in the wall of the cave closest to her, kneeling at once.

"We are so happy to find you here safe!" Ceddie flew to the boulder at her feet chirping in agreement.

"And you as well my friends, but where is here?" asked Madrena then added, "Please, stand," as she stroked the great bird's neck and back.

Night stood. "Where here is…is a good question, my princess; but I did overhear your mother say the name Rhetoric."

Madrena glanced down in thought briefly going through lessons learned, then said, "Rhetoric was my grandfathers' aide who later deceived him…one of evil's finest. Where he escaped to many years ago has never been revealed to me in my teachings but it must be near, never before have I seen such a world of blackness."

The dark faeries face became more serious and added, "Things are much worse outside the cave, Madrena. It is a wonder we found you. Cedrick and I are worried for you." "Do not worry," she tried to reply calmly, as she felt the vibrations of the trunk in her hand. It wanted her to open it and she wanted to. "Please, tell me how did you find me?" Night smiled and turned to reveal the Cane of Narzio that hung across his back in Day's sheath. Madrena recognized it immediately.

"You flew into your book?"

"Yes," answered Night. "Just as in the World of Dreams for Sam, do you remember? It was your mother who thought of using our book to find you." He barely paused, taking a quick excited breath. "Your father and she were the ones in need and we," he pointed at Ceddie and himself, "were the ones sent to help." He paused once more; you could see his eyes filling with even more amazement. "The book glowed brighter than I have ever seen it, my princess. It was incredible!"

The half smile appeared once more on her face and the eyebrow went up again. "Would this book glow too?" she thought then aloud asked, "And what message have you been sent to give me?"

Night smiled back, answering quickly. "Just like your mother, one step ahead!"

Her smile broke into a full one this time, "You have no idea!" she thought as he continued.

"However it is not a message, my dear princess but a riddle. One for your eyes only and then it must be destroyed. There it is, attached to Cedrick's leg."

Madrena looked over to the magnificent eagle that still sat on the boulder. Reaching down she stroked his neck once more, then loosened the paper attached to his leg with the single strand of leather. She started to unfold it but Cedrick's chirp stopped her and she looked up at him saying, "Yes Ceddie, I know, my eyes only."

The faerie princess turned picking up her necklace from the cave floor, double checking the emerald lid as she did; making sure it was closed then strapped it to Cedrick's leg with the single strand of leather.

"Please Ceddie, carry this with you; and Night, please, give this to my mother. Tell her all is well. I will be waiting for their arrival. Now, you must be on your way, I remember the rules of the trapdoor."

Night looked at her and Cedrick saw it too, their princess stood strong and straight. They saw no question in her eyes, she knew her place to be was here, on the inside. They were proud to call her princess. Night gave her a short bow and said, "Your mother said you would know where you were needed. Do not doubt your parents' belief in your strength and wisdom."

"I am my mother and father's daughter," she returned the bow to each of them, "I am what I am because of them, my ancestors and all my friends, like you; back home," she replied, humbly. ...And the dragonfly's eyebrows went up then down.

Cedrick squawked, signaling the need to go to Night, and he jumped up on the huge eagle's wing pulling the Cane of Narzio from his sister's sheath.

"Till we meet again my dear princess! Have no doubt we will find you once more!"

"Or me you!" she responded. Night smiled, Cedrick wished he could, and off they flew into the blackness outside of the cave.

Madrena walked to its mouth looking up into the sky for her friends but they were gone into the dark mist that seemed to rise from the very ground itself, mixing with the blackness of the sky to create a look of absolute nothingness. Why does the mist not enter this cave she wondered? She walked back into the body of the cave and looked down at the paper still folded in her hand. You could hear the paper crinkle as she opened it in the now silent cave, and a small tear ran down her cheek as she recognized her mother's writing. Quickly she wiped it away; this was no time for tears. Madrena was sure the adventure that lay before her would most definitely test the knowledge of all she had learned. She read on...

My dear Madrena,

On the night your grandfather faded he wrote down this riddle and gave me the emerald you now wear around your neck. He said there would come a time when your eyes only should read it. We believe that time is now!

Riddle me this
What is total bliss!
Riddle me that
That is made of slat!
Make no doubt
What's in or what's out…
For remember your lessons of yesteryear
…and look, oh yes! Within the tear!
We will find you…

Love Mom and Dad.

Madrena looked up from the paper tearing it quickly into a thousand pieces, burying them in the soft dirt of the cave. Slowly, she brought up her right hand, opening it to look at the trunk. It had been vibrating softly for the last few minutes and now there was a faint glow, just like the necklace and it felt somewhat larger than before. She stared at the trunk, marveling at the ornate carvings on its sides. Her eyes got wider as it faded from view then reappeared slightly larger and heavier.

"Oh my!" she barely whispered. A smile came across her face. "Trunks can have all kinds of things in them," she mused, setting it on the cavern floor. "But in my family they usually have books!" She took a step back, watching as the trunk began to fade in and out of view. Each time it reappeared, it became larger in size until it sat quiet as if waiting…the only glow coming from the latch itself.

"It wants me to open it." …and the young faerie princess wanted to open it but hesitated, going over the riddle again in her head. There was no doubt in her mind she was a step ahead in solving the meaning of it. No doubt in her mind that what was *'made of slat'* was this trunk. There was *'no doubt what is in or out'* for she was sure there was a book in there. *'Lessons of yesteryear'* told her that. …and that *'tear'* had been the emerald in her necklace where the trunk had been hidden. But what was *'total bliss'?* Could it be the book inside? Could it be the end of Rhetoric? Madrena placed her hands on the now full sized, ornately designed trunk. It hummed quietly as if feeling the same excitement and anticipation that she herself felt. …And the eyes of the dragonfly watched from the shadows. "You my dear, you are total bliss," he whispered.

As big and heavy as the lid looked, it was surprisingly light and opened without too much effort. Madrena leaned over the edge looking down at the book she knew would be there. Strangely, no title graced its cover she noticed, as she picked it up, tilted it out and blew the dust from it.

Gently she closed the lid of the trunk and set the book on top. No title…mmmh.

This could not be one of the books back in Whisper Hollow all of those have titles. She closed her eyes, thinking, remembering. Twelve books sat on the shelves back home, but thirteen had been saved by my father, as a knight would be magician. Opening her eyes the excitement showed plainly, not one but both eyebrows at their highest. This must be the thirteenth book, the one my grandfather hid himself!

Madrena lightly touched her neck and smiled, all this time it had been right here. Over the years she had learned that this thirteenth book could be opened by both Good and Evil. That with it one could rewrite the other twelve; hence her grandfather's great care in hiding it, but she had been forbidden to talk of it. This is the book evil wants, for with it, all thirteen could be used by evil for evil.

She wanted to open it, even the book seemed to want her to open it! A soft glow now came from the pages. She turned glancing around the cavern seeing nothing at all, thinking. I did not come here knowingly; someone brought me. If that someone was evil it would be trying to get the book now, before she herself could open it. Her eyes once more glanced around the cavern and saw nothing. Madrena turned back to the book, took a deep breath and slowly lifted the cover. ... And the dragonfly tensed, drawing in a deep breath also as she did.

Faded parchment paper glowed softly in the minimal cavern light allowing her to read the writing that immediately filled the page.

Are you Adren?

scrawled out the book. "No," she said aloud without thinking and turned the page.

Are you Good or Evil?

appeared almost as fast as the first question. "Good... always!" she answered turning yet another page. Again the first question,

Are you Adren?

Madrena opened her mouth to answer once more but a voice from somewhere behind her spoke first, "No, she is not, I am."

She froze, turning slowly, her wings spreading in preparation of what could happen and looked directly into the eyes of an oversized dragonfly, a very beautiful one. Their eyes met as it hovered only inches from her face.

She was not afraid. "And who is Adren might I ask?"

The dragonfly fanned its brightly colored wings moving itself backwards. Madrena felt the light wind they created move the loose tendrils of her braid. It fell briefly into the shadows of the cave, and then reemerged having transformed into a faerie standing a full head taller than she. His eyes were penetrating and her heart beat fast.

She swallowed taking a deep breath at the same time and said, "Who are you?"

He answered almost immediately, his eyes never leaving hers. "You are my destiny and I yours." Her right eyebrow went up and he continued with a smile. "You are very much like your father with that eyebrow."

Her eyes squinted at the remark. "You know him?" she asked.

The handsome dragonfly faerie blinked his eyes, "Let us turn another page."

"And why should I trust you at my back?" Madrena asked turning, eyes locked with his until she was forced to face the book.

His answer was simple. He whispered it in her ear, "Because you can."

A warm chill filled her with his answer, the good kind. Her fingers touched a corner of the page, lifting it slightly as she thought of his breath and the way it had felt against her skin. Adren…Adren…she remembered no Adren from her teachings. The message was waiting as the page fell back.

"And you must be Madrena!"

"Yes! But how?" This time she did not have to turn the page, the book scrawled the answer instantly…

"Your Grandfather!"

Madrena turned from the book now and faced the dragon-fly turned faerie named Adren, searching his eyes. "You must know more than I do, please tell me everything so that I may put some pieces together with what I already know."

He responded by taking her hands into his. "First, let me know that you believe I am not here to harm you, only to help."

His eyes filled her and something deep inside her stirred. She did not know why but she did believe him, and "I believe you," tumbled from her mouth. His hands came up to her shoulders and he squeezed slightly. "Two years before your father Enol defeated evil as a knight would be magician, your grandfather visited the land in which I come from, Anisoptera."

"Land of the Dragonfly," she broke in.

"Yes," he answered.

"I have heard of this place. You are half faerie, half dragon-fly?" Madrena asked.

He bowed. "You do not approve?"

"Oh no, I like how you fit together!" Madrena's hand went up covering her mouth instantly. "I'm sorry. Sometimes things just come out of my mouth." Her hands went to her cheeks, she was blushing she could feel the heat!

He answered, "Thank you, no problem and I like the way you look, too!"

They both laughed and Adren continued, "After your grand-father spent some time in our village, he approached my father and mother, Anales and Anora, both accomplished warriors saying that he had a vision of them. He told a story of the future to my parents, a story of the possible end of life in Anisoptera, and all other Faerie worlds, as we know it. A story of how evil would once again try to control us all through the thirteenth book."

Madrena twisted around, a "WOW" whispering from her mouth as she gazed down at the book then back at Adren. She was right, it was the thirteenth book.

He continued, "Your grandfather then told my parents of the son they would have in one year's time." The dragonfly faerie bowed slightly, smiling then continued again. "He requested I be trained to be a better warrior than our land had ever seen. I do not know if I am all that, but I think we will find out in the near future."

Madrena thought mmmh, modesty. I like that. She broke in, "How did you get here…to this cave…and how do you know my parents?"

"I think your grandfather knowing of me, and what the future held somehow linked me with the book…I think."

He nodded toward the book at her back, and she glanced around at it. "I had dreams for many nights, dreams of a girl… you. Dreams of the book, dreams of a gray haired older man who told me to believe, and dreams of a dark place, this cave I believe. I left Anisoptera and found myself in Whisper Hollow. From a nearby limb outside your home, I saw the great hawk Ceddie arrive, your father; the two faces in the tree, Id and Odd and of course you."

"How come it is that you did not speak up and make yourself known when you were there?" Madrena asked.

"My destiny is you alone. My dreams told me this is where we would first meet." Adren glanced around the cave and the rocks overhead. Madrena's eyes however stayed looking straight at him until he returned the stare.

"But how did you get to this cave?" She tilted her head to the right, squinting at him, continuing before he could answer, "…how did I get here?"

"I carried you."

Madrena stared at him, almost mad, almost, but the glow from behind her made them both turn to look at the book. The pages were glowing once more, and the next page had turned itself! Instantly across the page words scrawled themselves,

"It is time!"

"Time for what?" asked Madrena glancing back at Adren, who responded quickly.

"I have told you all I know, the rest we will learn together. Please, turn another page." …And she did.

Both their eyes grew wide as the page drew a picture of a beautiful place resting on what seemed to be a large cloud. Adren looked from the book to Madrena catching a look of familiarity crossing her face, as silent words escaped quietly through her lips.

"Do you know this place?" he asked.

"Yes, but," Madrena stood back looking hard at the picture. The twisted pines were unmistakable, she was sure they existed nowhere else.

"What, what do you see?" he repeated.

"The place I am thinking of is gone, unreachable, gone," she said as she threw her hands into the air then placed them on her hips. "It can't be, can it?"

"Can't be what?" asked Adren. The faerie princess looked up at him and once more back at the page, "Quiviera."

He leaned over Madrena's shoulder looking deeper into the picture. "What is this place, Quiviera?"

"The home of my grandfather and grandmother, named after them both. The Q-u-i was for Quinn and the v-i-e-r-a for Saviera, hence Quiviera. This could not possibly be it. It faded away when grandfather did. Just faded away as if it never existed and it never sat on a cloud."

"Well this book seems to think it does, or remembers it somehow," Adren replied still looking deep into the picture, his eyes focused on one particular spot. "Madrena, look over here," he pointed just to the right of center. "What do you see there? Is that something moving?"

Slow to answer, she was marveling at the similarities, double checking her guess that it truly was Quiviera. "Where?"

"There," said Adren pointing now at the base of one of the biggest twisted pines in the picture. Sure enough, something was moving, but it was so small they could not make it out.

Madrena looked up and smiled at Adren. "Please don't think of me as forward, but I must put my hand in yours if you are to see what I see."

Her hand slipped softly into his, he smiled. She placed her other hand on the picture just above the moving object, and they both saw.

An old man stood waving with his right hand, the left one gripped a knotted wood cane that help support him and he was smiling. Madrena was beside herself wanting to scream out to her grandfather but knew he would not be able to hear her for there were limits to her magic. She looked over at Adren and saw the look of surprise on his face as he said, "Do you know this man?"

"Yes, he is my grandfather, but he cannot hear or see us." She stared at him seeing the trees and grass behind him, through him; and added, "I wonder why he is so transparent?"

He placed a hand on her arm making her hesitate, "He is the man from my dreams and was just as transparent in them." The faerie princess looked from him to her grandfather briefly, "Let's get back."

Back once more in the cave, standing again in front of the

book, Madrena took her hand from his but not before he gave it one quick squeeze, their eyes meeting briefly.

"So your grandfather lives?" Adren asked.

She turned gazing down at the book. "His appearance seems to be more in a spirit form, but I'm not sure, maybe some part of him lives within the book." She paused, her eyes shining with wonder. "The power of this book is amazing!" Her finger traced the outer edge of the book as she marveled a little longer; adding, "Nothing more has been written on the page, maybe we should turn it?"

Adren nodded, "Yes, I agree."

Three words scrawled quickly on the page as Madrena let it fall.

"Quiviera Awaits You!"

Her mind was racing in anticipation of what the book had in mind. What was it? She looked at Adren and turned the page. Immediately the same picture they had already seen drew itself once more on the page. Underneath two more words were scrawled.

"Dive in!"

Adren could just get out, "Do you think?"

"Yes," answered Madrena simply. "I do. Night and Day, two of the faeries in Whisper Hollow dove into their book, but they needed the Cane of Narzio to get out. You may have seen the cane earlier from your hiding place where it hung on the wall back home." She flashed him a sassy smirk followed by a mischievous grin and he smiled back. "Actually I saw it here for the first time earlier."

Adren moved to Madrena's side and turned her, making them face to face. "You talk of lessons learned; well in mine your grandfather is the author of the last twelve, inspired by the first created, the thirteenth. Is that how you learned it?"

"Yes but the thirteenth had a title, The Book of Anisoptera, this one has none." She quickly flipped back the cover, not losing their page, and both were amazed to find that it now had a title.

"It was not there earlier!" Madrena blurted.

"No. It was not," agreed Adren; adding, "Maybe, just maybe, the book was protecting itself. You know, until it was sure of who was opening it." He paused briefly, seeing agreement in her eyes as she turned to look directly in his eyes, and he added, "Would you not agree that the thirteenth is the most powerful of them all?"

"Yes," she answered.

His response was quick. "Then we should do as the book asks."

Her mind was racing again as she stared back down at it. She thought of her mother and father, of Whisper Hollow and the faeries there who were counting on her to do whatever was needed…but what if they could not get back out of the book? She stared once more at the open book, the page and the invite to dive in.

"In all my teachings one thing has been stressed the most… Believe! Believe in the power of the books." Her eyes never left it. Yes, they must believe in the power of the books. She must believe in the power of this book.

Adren saw her mind working as her eyes stared at the picture. "I think Quinn, your grandfather; will be glad to see us." He gently placed his hand on her chin turning her face to his. "Ready?" He smiled seeing the excitement that once again sparkled in her eyes as she turned to look into his. One word was all she spoke, "Yes!"

…And with that Madrena and Adren took each others hands; and without hesitation spread their wings, and flew up then down into the picture believing most assuredly in the power of this thirteenth book.

* * *

The large raven soared high above Whisper Hollow, and the home of Enol, Ciera, Madrena and the faeries of Whisper Hollow; he was a full day ahead of his comrades. His mind swam with thoughts of the promises that had been made to him by Rhetoric, himself; promises that would be kept only once the trunk and the thirteenth book were in his possession.

His eyes narrowed seeing the five faerie soldiers standing below. He could take them all, he was sure of it. The raven dove down just to the treetops, hiding his large size behind the most outer layers of leaves. For nearly an hour he had watched the five, seeing no one leave or enter the house. Why had Rhetoric sent us all? Did these five fight that well? Would it take us all to defeat them? He wondered all these things and more, and in the end decided it was not for him to decide.

CHAPTER V

...And So It Begins

CIERA, ENOL, and the others had left Whisper Hollow immediately. Sneakin, Night and Piggett had expressed their worries of leaving the books, before they did.

"The books are held to the shelf as you guys know by magic. Magic passed down by Quinn, Ciera's father and his ancestors. Eighteen of your fellow faeries including Fire and Smoke, along with Emmit and his men, will be here to guard them," Enol had answered quickly. However his face had still shown the same concern they had. A grunt from behind, caused him to turn around. Fire and Smoke, who both did not look well, stood there, visibly trying to maintain balance. "Are you two okay?" asked Enol.

Smoke nodded yes then no and Fire spoke for them both. "Woke up this morning feeling weak, kind of, not normal, you know."

Ciera stepped forward testing their foreheads, "No fever but you do have a pale look about you. Both of you will stay here, in our home with the books."

"Yes," Enol added, memories of their fading book had flashed through his head, "Stay here."

They and their small troop left then, leaving them both on the couch with blankets and hot tea, both watching Day as she waited for her brother and Cedrick's return. Emmit and his men had stationed themselves outside, and the other fairies had returned home to rest and ready themselves for their turn to watch over the books.

They were just now entering Amberwood. Only the sounds of their footsteps and the occasional clink of weaponry against their bodies, as they walked, could be heard. Not even Piggett, Skinny, and Hyde made a sound as they scrambled ahead of the group in the tall grass bordering the trail.

Enol leaned over, whispering to Ciera, almost making her jump as she was awakened from her thoughts about the present she had left on Madrena's pillow; the one with the triscale and thirteen emeralds, the one passed down from her mother to her, meant for Madrena. It was very old. The triscale symbol in front, a sacred one of their ancestors, was topped by a single emerald, with six more scattered artistically on either side.

"Haven't heard one chirp from one bird in a while...you?"

"No, I have not," she answered, quickly searching the area around them as she raised her hand and all behind came to a stand still. Silence filled the air, all eyes going from their surroundings to each other, then back to the trees and grasses at their sides. Suddenly, a whirring sound filled the silence and blades of grass shot, not flew; up into the air all around them. The sound stopped as leaves fell down upon them from the treetops above. Sneakin started to say something but Ciera stopped him. She was smiling as she held her finger to her mouth and winked at him. She called out, "Faeries of

Amberwood, it is I, Ciera; your Queen. Please show yourself for your help is needed."

For a moment the silence continued, but then a rustling could be heard; and the green faeries of Amberwood seemed to appear out of the very leaves on the trees surrounding them. What they lacked in wings, they made up with the ability to tumble, climb and blend and they showed their skills; tumbling to the ground with expert flips and curls as they made their way from branch to branch slowly to the forest floor below.

Ciera leaned over close to her husband whispering, "They are said to have webbed feet and hands giving them excellent gripping abilities."

Enol was amazed saying, "All these years I have lived less than a day's travel from this place, and never been aware of them, much less this place."

The tallest of them, just up to his waist, stepped forward. "But we have always known of you Enol. We are honored." An eyebrow rose in recognition of his name. The light green faerie continued, as he turned toward Ciera bowing ever so slightly. "My Queen, we are at your service. How may we help?"

Ciera looked around at the five faeries that had emerged. They were armed with bows and arrows, and daggers hung on most of their hips. "The books are in danger and our daughter Madrena is missing."

There was no hesitation by the green faerie, his reply automatic. "What is our destination, my Queen?"

"The Fortress of Rhetoric," she replied.

Again no hesitation from the green fairy, "We will prepare." He turned to go, but turned back when Enol spoke. "And your name my new friend?"

"I am Tarin, leader of this small group," he answered with a wave toward the others. Enol held out his hand and they shook. "I look forward to getting to know you better, Tarin."

Ciera reached out placing her hand lightly on the faeries shoulder. "One question sir, the Wind Riders, have you seen them?"

Tarin turned and pointed at one of his troop who sat on a long, thin outstretched twig in a tree nearby. "This is Maurie, daughter of Maran, Leader of the Wind Riders. As you can see, she is light as a feather. She does not, as of yet, possess the same abilities to ride the wind as her father. He was here just last week, and usually returns every other week to visit."

"A week is too long to wait Tarin, is there a way to contact him and the others?" asked Ciera.

"With your help, my Queen; I believe their might be. I have heard you can read thoughts and send them….yes?" he asked, his eyebrow rising.

"Yes, but the Wind Riders are not faeries; in fact, they are merely air that has taken form." Ciera turned to look at Maurie, her eyes squinting, her mouth now forming a smile, an eyebrow rising and she continued. "There is a common link though, her mother. Was she a member of your group?"

"Yes. She died in childbirth. What ever is in that form that air has taken in the way of the Wind Riders, it was too much for her to give birth to."

"She looks to be full faerie," said Ciera, still looking over at Maurie, taking a step toward her.

Tarin walked toward the young faerie, gently lifting her chin, saying, "You can tell when you look at her eyes, who her father is."

…And you could. Maurie's blue eyes were large, and they showed the wind that blew continually behind them. Ciera placed a hand gently on the young faeries head; it was worth a try. They would absolutely need the Wind Riders help.

"Close your eyes, dear."

In only seconds those huge blue eyes sprang back open, larger than before, showing the wind once more. "It worked!" blurted Maurie. "I could feel my father's presence! I could not see him but I could feel him!"

Ciera smiled back at her, nodding in agreement.

Tarin stepped backwards one step, bowing, "My Queen, we will ready ourselves."

Ciera turned to him, quick to respond, "Please…we must leave within the hour. There is much ground to cover in order to reach the Forest of Fire by noon tomorrow and before we make camp for the night."

Enol turned to Sneakin who stood just behind him, knowing instantly the same two words were echoing in his head as well…*Forest of Fire?* Enol smiled saying, "I suppose we will be seeing many new places on our quest, my friend. Tell the others to rest while they can."

The tallest faerie in Whisper Hollow smiled back. "Yes sir, I am sure we will." He snapped his wing, and with a nod of his head turned to tell the others, his sword swinging ever so slightly as he did.

Sunck flew up to Enol, "My sister, brother and I must go back to the pond we passed not so long ago. The water calls!" As water faeries, they had to maintain a certain level of water within themselves.

Enol nodded, "Not a problem, but do not take to long; and look for Night and Day, they should be catching up with us, hopefully with good news!"

Sunck warbled a "See you soon!" and he, his brother and sister, Saynk and Cinq, flew off back toward the water they needed.

Enol's face got serious as he turned towards Ciera. She was as worried as he was, but the half smiles appeared and the serious looks of both faded somewhat when a familiar screech was heard from above just moments later. Cedrick flew down, landing on a limb next to them. Night and Day both jumped from his wing, as he did.

"Mission accomplished! Madrena has the riddle!"

"Good job, you three!" said Enol with Ciera nodding in agreement, as she stroked the great bird's neck.

"Please tell me of this place where she is. What is it like?" she asked.

Night was hesitant in answering, not wanting to worry his queen but wanting still to be truthful.

Day twisted her head around toward her brother peering at him as if urging him with her eyes, finally saying what she was thinking, "Night, tell her. She needs to know. They both have a right to know."

The small dark faerie nodded agreeing and turned to Ciera. "It is not a good place, my queen," he paused, "Blackness surrounds her. However she is inside a cave, and seems to be fine. It is outside the cave that scares me. There seems to be no ground below, nor sky above. A dark mist seems to rise from somewhere obscuring what is really there."

Ciera's eyes narrowed. "It is said that the land surrounding Rhetoric's Fortress is filled with a black pitch spewed forth out of his very body."

"There are two more things we should tell you," spoke up Night. "First, your daughter seemed older somehow, stronger than I have ever seen her. She reminded us of you, my Queen, always one step ahead of us."

Cedrick chirped in agreement, and held up his leg revealing to her the necklace. Ciera removed it, smiling as she touched the emerald lightly, popping its lid open, seeing what she had known she would see…an empty compartment. She snapped it shut again, and looked over at Enol whose eyes questioned the necklace's presence, and the compartment inside he had never known anything about.

"Our daughter is fine, my husband; and getting smarter all along."

"I have never seen her necklace off, ever," he said.

"Think of it as a good sign, my dear," responded Ciera, quickly turning back to Night, "And the second thing?"

Before he could answer, a breeze kicked up, blowing Ciera's hair to one side of her face, as she touched Enol's hand. The Wind Riders had arrived!

Enol stood frozen, still staring at Night, "And the second thing?" he repeated.

Night lowered his eyes now and glanced over at Day and Cedrick, "When we came back, back through the book…well, it was as if the darkness jumped or reached out from the pages of the book, as if it was grabbing for us; that it did not want to release us…"

Enol turned to his wife, their eyes meeting their thoughts the same. "His powers are getting stronger."

"Yes, we must talk to the Wind Riders and be on our way." Both turned together, their eyes once again filled with concern for their daughter and the fairies that accompanied them.

* * *

Air that has simply taken form is the only way to describe a Wind Rider. While definition and facial features could be seen, they were still simply made up of air. Having no wings, they simply rode the wind itself like a dry leaf but with control. Maran, leader of the three, stepped down an invisible step from a wind that gently swirled the leaves close to his feet, causing their hair and clothes to blow softly, then stood before Enol and Ciera.

Maurie, his daughter ran up, hugging him. He smiled at her, then turned his gaze back to them and spoke with a gravelly voice. "Queen of all Faeries, what can I do for you."

"It is time for Rhetoric's demise," replied Ciera simply.

"Really..." Maran said nodding toward Enol then back to Ciera. He continued, "I have heard stories only of the path to Rhetoric's Fortress, none good. A path full of tricks and traps only the evil of Rhetoric could think of. Did you bring your biggest bag of magic my Faerie Queen? For you will need it."

Nip for the first time showed his face on her shoulder, gnashing his teeth in support of her. Ciera pet him and smiled, "Be assured, Wind Rider; we have come prepared. Your presence will be needed once we are within sight of Rhetorics fortress. Two rivers meet there, the Zacarra and the Tube."

The gravelly voice came again, "I know the spot how is it that you think we can help?"

Maran saw the sparkle in her eye as she said, "Clear the air," and he admired it without doubt of her bravery. He had heard of her adventures and triumphs with evil over the years. There was no telling what this beautiful queen had up her sleeve.

"Mmhh! We will meet then, where the Zacarra and Tube meet. How long will it take you to get there, Ciera?"

She responded quickly, "We will arrive by mid afternoon on the fourth day; you will be needed on the morning of the fifth."

"So be it then, five days." His eyes turned briefly upwards scanning the sky. "Until then, we must ride the wind directing it where it is most needed." Maran turned to his daughter, brushing her cheek gently. "It was good seeing you so soon Maurie. Will you follow Ciera?"

"Yes, my father." Her big eyes looked up to his and he smiled at the sight of the wind inside.

"You, my dear; have a destiny; as with everything, you were created for a reason. Take care, and know that your mother would be very proud of you." Maran held up a finger feeling the upcoming wind. He turned to Ciera and Enol nodding and spoke as he stepped up on that invisible step again. "You can count on us." …And off they went. Everyone watched as they left. They were quite the sight to see as they swooped and dove, in and out of clouds directing the winds of the world.

Ciera broke the silence. "Tarin, are your people ready?"

"Whenever you are, my Queen," he said with a nod, hoisting his bow in the air to signal the other four faeries to ready themselves.

Ciera stepped up onto a flat topped boulder, glancing toward Enol who held up a hand signaling all the others. The sudden commotion caused Tuck to run through the folds in her wrap, in search of a better place to sleep. It tickled, almost making her giggle aloud. She patted her furry friend affectionately then returned her attention to the others.

"We will camp tonight at the edge of a world most of you have never known," She turned and smiled at Enol briefly and continued, squeezing his hand a little harder. "…and I promise you a good story. One never heard before!"

Enol played along, recognizing that whispery voice and the squeezing of the hand, she was teasing him. It was the truth though, she had always told better stories, even he knew that. "Are you saying I tell *bad* stories? Because I don't." He glanced in the direction of Whisper Hollow's tallest faerie then back over at his wife. "Tell them Sneak have you ever fallen asleep during one of *my* stories?"

"Just once, sir," came back quickly. Enol looked back at the faerie, his own eyebrow raised and they all laughed aloud.

* * *

They were seventeen strong now, with Night, Day and the five Amberwood faeries and that would be twenty once they reached

Rhetorics' Fortress counting the Wind Riders, if they all survived the journey that lay before them. Each member of the troop had different abilities; all would have different purposes in their quest of Rhetoric, and the success of their mission.

Together, Ciera and Enol had decided it best to leave the soldier faeries, along with Fire and Smoke, and the others in Whisper Hollow. The books must be protected. There had been some protests from the ones that had been left, no surprise. They wanted to be with their Queen and knight magician, aiding in the destruction of Rhetoric, and be the soldier and warrior faeries they were intended to be. Enol had explained, "That is exactly what you will be doing. By guarding these books, you prevent them from being stolen by Rhetoric for their magic and most importantly, you protect the faeries attached to them." In the end, eighteen faeries and the soldier faeries had reluctantly stayed to protect the books at all cost. Should they have brought more help?

That thought was shared by all, I think, as they continued down the path to the edge of the only world they had ever known, towards the edge of a world they had never known. They pushed forward, toward Rhetoric, and his fortress of evil.

CHAPTER VI

IBNot

THEY MADE their camp that night in a hollow under fir trees, hung with a moss called logger's beard. Long, silvery and gray in color it was motionless, moving only when caught on the slight breeze that came up from time to time.

Cinq, Saynk, and Sunck had placed their tent over the top of two rocks above the creek that trickled calmly, giving them dry land, yet the water they loved and must have. Piggett, Skinny, and Hyde were further out on a soft bed of fresh needles that had fallen from the trees above. While Night and Day chose higher up, balancing their tent on the tip of a great bough hanging just to the side of the fire built by Sneakin and Peakin, and where their tent was…well, only they knew.

Enol and Ciera had placed their tent on a knoll of clover where the morning light would shine first. Not far, two fallen trees over grown with moss crossed the creek, creating a bridge that led to a shadowed area beyond. In the fading light of day, you could just see the split wood wedged between two trees probably when they were but saplings by a traveler of long ago. Now so absorbed in the growth of the trees themselves, that it formed a bench of sorts...this is where the faeries of Amberwood had set up their tents.

Ciera took all this in as she sat close to their tent and looked out over the small camp from faerie to faerie. All were proven adventurers, all with accomplished fighting skills of their own. She smiled as they laughed around the fire, telling their stories of the past, and of lessons learned. Gazing momentarily at her husband she thought of Madrena briefly, wondering how she was, while her eyes continued their wandering. Following the high embankment surrounding the hollow in which they had camped, she concentrated momentarily on the twisted and gnarled roots of the trees above as they fell to the valley floor.

Enol saw the deep thought on her face. "What is it, my dear?"

Ciera glanced quickly over at him, giving him a wink and nodded towards their comrades. "It is time to tell a story."

The Queen of all Faeries stood, walking over to the edge of the knoll and sat down again cross legged, absorbing the warmth of the fire in the cool night air. She scanned her comrades once more as they chatted and laughed, catching bits and pieces of their conversations. Sneakin, Saynk and Night seemed to be arguing over where Madrena had been taken; while two of their female counterparts, Peakin and Day floated just above the outreached arm of a huge fern, discussing the changing powers of the books.

Cinq and Sunck splashed in the clear water creek at her feet, just below their tent. From their remarks, she could tell they were listening to the other two conversations and stating their own opinions. Tarin, Maurie and the other three faeries of Amberwood sat quietly hearing all this as they sharpened their daggers and tested their crossbows.

She turned her gaze on Enol now, who looked up at her at nearly the same time, and she winked at him again, blowing him a kiss. Peakin looked down from Day just in time to see that kiss and smiled, thinking, "They are so in love, so devoted to each other."

Ciera's eyes came up to meet hers instantly, and Peakin heard her say, "Yes, we are," without one movement of her Queens' mouth. The young faerie put her hands to her face, feeling the heat of the blush upon her cheeks. Ciera gave her a smile, once again scanning the group, silently summoning their attention without a word and they heard.

All quieted, the only thing to be heard now was Odd's snoring, which immediately stopped when Cedrick flew over landing on the closest branch to the face and chirped loudly, waking him.

Their Queen sat silent just for the moment, that familiar half smile on her face, eyes alive and sparkling.

"You have all come here not really knowing what the next danger will be in this endeavor to protect the books and save Madrena. Enol and I thank you for that."

Sneakin broke in with the familiar snap of his wing. "Ciera, no reasons were needed for she is our princess, as you are our queen. We have watched her grow…we have grown because of her."

The other faeries all nodded in agreement and Peakin spoke up, "I was taught that on the day I die if I could count five friends on one hand I would be truly very lucky…all of us are that lucky for we can all count more than six times that amount." She spread her arms to encompass all of them, adding, "We are family, Madrena is part of that family. There was never a question of not coming."

Again, all nodded in agreement and Ciera smiled as did Enol. However, her face did not hold the smile instead it grew more serious as she said, "Then, know this my friends and comrades, and beware, for I tell you a story tonight of a living creature relentless in his search for the thirteenth book. A creature brought to life by Rhetoric out of the very pitch that spews from his own body, and now surrounds his fortress. His name is IBNot."

She paused noticing the total focus they had upon her, and then continued. "Not one drop of good blood runs through its veins, if it has veins. IBNot, like my Cedrick; is the eyes and ears of Rhetoric himself. Many times since my father passed away I have seen this creature, but only, from the corner of my eye. He is a spy sent by Rhetoric himself to find the thirteenth book. Forever at my back should I reveal its location, and will be at Madrena's back one day. He waits in the shadows under the fern or the gnarled roots of the hillside trees." She paused briefly, looking up at the embankment, causing them all to do the same, then continued, "Just out of sight till he is summoned by Rhetoric to do his bidding."

Cinq swam to a nearby twig and propped herself up almost halfway out of the creek. When Ciera paused, she asked in her watery voice, "This thirteenth book, my Queen; has it ever been opened?"

Ciera smiled at the question, and brought her hand up to her throat touching Madrena's necklace she now wore around her own neck. "I think it has been by now."

Enol watched as his wife's hand stroked their daughter's necklace and put two and two together. Ciera glanced at him, hearing his thoughts. "Yes," she replied without words, "The book was meant for Madrena all along."

Gasps could be heard from the others as Enol realized his wife had not just been talking in his head, but in everyone's. She continued mouth unmoving and all were silent and listened closely as she did. "Rhetoric thru IBNot could be and probably is listening even now, so important things need not be said aloud. His evil mission has and will always be to find the thirteenth book. We must be discreet. If Rhetoric were to find out that the thirteenth book is meant for Madrena, and she is right now in his possession…"

The Queen of all Faeries lowered her head momentarily then raised it her eyes now shining like blue fire. "IBNot, along with Rhetoric himself must be destroyed." Their queen paused again, swallowing, taking a deep breath, continuing once more. "IBNot, my friends; comes from an ancient tribe of people called Chameleons, so called this because of their ability to blend into any background. This will allow Rhetoric to know our plans, and to know each step we take. Do not doubt for one minute that he is not out there, even now. However there is hope. This nocturnal tribe could only be stopped by the first light of the morning star on the fifth day of Venus. It was deadly to them, as it would be to IBNot. Today my friends, ironically was the first day of those five days of Venus. We must take full advantage of this, and rid ourselves of the evil IBNot so we may concentrate on Rhetoric!" All nodded, understanding and remained quiet but their Queen and Enol smiled as they heard their thoughts of "Yes!"

"One last thing, Madrena can take care of herself," she paused looking towards Enol. "I am sure of it." He would never tell anyone about the glimmer of a tear that showed itself at that very moment and then was gone. The bravest woman he knew turned back towards the others and added aloud, "For now we must worry about ourselves and getting through to Rhetoric's Fortress safely." Ciera smiled at them all, as she stood and stretched, then walked back to her husband, resting her head on his shoulder. All were quiet as thoughts of all they had just learned sunk in, when Peakin let out a big yawn reminding them all, that sleep was indeed needed.

Goodnights were said as everyone but Sneak, who had first watch, retired for the night.

* * *

The roots of the trees on the hillside, just above their camp twisted down and around and around and down each other again and again. In fact, they were intertwined so much that at certain levels, they could not be distinguished from each other. The moss, the green ivy and the natural paling of the wood, only added to their beauty.

Enol was enjoying his coffee, and he had got up early to have it. Ciera, as always, would be ready to go upon waking, there would be no time for coffee then…and he did like his coffee. He poured the last of it into his cup from the pot on the fire, and turned toward the tent, reaching for the flap, but his hand never touched it; his face sobering as he turned back towards that hillside. Chills ran up his back with a gut wrenching feeling. The feeling of being watched by someone, suddenly churned inside him. His eyes scanned the eerily quiet forest, and glanced from tent to tent, seeing or hearing no movement.

Once more his gaze fell upon the dangling roots, but this time he was not marveling at their beauty. He tried once more to follows the twists and turns of the roots examining the spaces between them. Was something there just out of his view?

"Yes," whispered an answer from behind him. Enol turned to see his wife standing, holding the flap to the tent open as she added, "It's been there all night."

"IBNot?" questioned Enol.

"Without a doubt," she answered.

He stared at her, his face serious. "Is our Madrena strong enough to withstand him if need be?" he asked.

Ciera's lips tightened, gazing at the ground momentarily and answered, "My powers have always been limited, limited to opposites, as in good and bad, living and dead. This is not so with our daughter, dear." Ciera let the tent flap go, gesturing to the world around them. "I draw power from the land, the plants and the animals, and my ancestors in times of great need. Madrena draws her power from the very air surrounding her. I learned from my father on the day of her birth how powerful she would be. Her powers may not yet be fully developed but she has enough understanding of them to succeed. Yes, she is quite capable of defeating him or will be."

Enol walked toward her, "Good," he said as he set down his coffee cup, and kissed her. "We should get going. I'll wake the others," he continued, their foreheads still touching. When he tried to go though Ciera held him firm.

"What? No more coffee?" she teased.

Enol showed his half grin, "Had two cups that's enough!" He lovingly traced her nose with a finger giving her one more, quick kiss and looked deep into her eyes letting her see the way he loved her and she returned the look.

They were so wrapped up in that stare that both physically jumped when someone from behind them cleared their throat announcing themselves.

"I am sorry to disturbed you both," started Sneakin with a glance back at the others, "but my comrades out here voted and I was elected to tell you we were here and ready as you requested."

Enol looked at Ciera with a '*did you call them?*' look.

"Nope," she answered but stopped abruptly looking at him, you know, with that queer kind of wondering kind of look.

His eyes tensed, questioning her. "What?"

"I think you called them, dear," Ciera answered as she broke into a smile. "In fact I am beginning to believe I shared more than years with you the way you seem to hear Cedrick; and now the way you simply stated that you would call the others and you did it, not even knowing it." She paused and looked at Sneakin. "Who called you, who did you hear?"

The reply came quickly. "Why you, sir," he answered, nodding at Enol.

Ciera smiled at him. "This could come in handy down the road."

Her husband's eyebrow rose and the half smile played on his lips as he turned towards the others. "Okay my friends, time to go!"

* * *

A dark figure stood hunched beside the table. The cape it wore embedded at the neckline into its very skin under the glistening smoke colored torque, draping to the floor around him, the bottom edge seeming to ooze a murky mist that covered what was the floor. From behind you could see the scarred hands that flipped furiously through the pages of the book before him. Black lines, with a movement almost all their own, traced along the knuckles, up his fingers, then his hands, then his arms, disappearing up under the cape. He was becoming the mist more and more every hour, every day; but he cared not, as his thoughts were not of the lines or the mist, but of the book and its empty pages.

His wings flared, showing the clipped portions that prevented flight; and he slammed it shut sending it sliding off the table at the feet of the faeries attached to it. Fire and Smoke were both remembering the day before, saying their goodbyes to Enol, Ciera and the others when it hit the floor, and it startled them somewhat…and then it spoke.

"How is it that you are here? How is it that you come here with this book?" His voice was deep and gurgled as he spoke through the pitch that filled his body.

The taller of the two faeries, Fire; stood straight, defiant, even though both their arms and legs were outstretched and chained to the wall above and below them. "Who wants to know?" he stated with a matter of fact tone in his voice.

The grotesque creature let out a grunt, and grabbed his jaw, its face mere inches away. "I am surprised as a member of Whisper Hollow that you do not know, that is, if you truly do not." His head dipped to the side as he spoke allowing a drip of pitch to splash to the ground; he cared not, and he kept going. "I'll play. I am Rhetoric." He moved closer, nearly nose to nose with Fire, adding, "The boogeyman in all of your ghost stories around the campfire at home in Whisper Hollow. The demon that scares you awake at night. I am Rhetoric the one whom you will now serve or die."

It was Smoke who spoke up then, causing Rhetoric to swing around toward him, dripping more pitch from the corner of his mouth, slinging it on the floor to his right. "We serve no man or faerie. We serve only the book."

The blackened face continued staring at him, his head slowing turning from him to the book and back. "So you serve the book," he gurgled, taking a moment to swallow the pitch welling up inside him. "Tell me then! Tell me how it works! How do I harness the power within it?"

Smoke said nothing, instead he leaned his head back, laughing aloud and turned to his brother. "Hey Fire, do I have 'magician' written on my forehead?"

The answer from Fire came quickly, "Nope! Do I?" he smiled.

Smoke turned a now serious face back to Rhetoric. "No you do not." He tightened his lips, staring straight into the black eyes of the creature standing before him stating, "And if we did we would still not tell you that answer."

Rhetoric raged, slapping him with an open fist, leaving pitch on his cheek. "Rot here for all I care! I will figure it out and you will serve me in the end." He reached out grabbing the hook that served as a handle on the door of the turret room. It slammed behind him. Both faeries looked down at their book that lay just at their feet, yet out of reach for either of them because of the shackles.

Fire spoke first, "They will come for us you know."

Smoke glanced over at his brother while wiping the pitch left on his cheek by Rhetoric on the shoulder of his shirt. His eyes settled on their book, then turned upward examining the walls around them. The turret room was at best twenty feet in circumference, which was good. Windows could barely be seen far above, windows filled with a gray black mist. If they could manage to get loose, flight might be possible. They were not as tall as their friend Sneakin, but their wingspan was the same. Gathering the amount of air they would need to lift them up the turret might be tough but both agreed they could probably do it. Smoke then turned his eyes toward the opposite wall of the turret.

"What are you looking for?" asked Fire.

"More shackles for our friends," he responded.

"Why?" came back fast.

Smoke looked over to his brother now, "Because he does not only want our book, he wants them all."

Fire pursed his lips, scanning the walls as well. It was a lot darker now that Rhetoric had closed the door completely, but his eyes were adjusting. No, there were no other shackles. "Enol said before they left, that he had seen our book fade."

Smoke's answer was quick, "Yes, as I am sure others are now, or already have." "Agreed," answered Fire simply. The corners of his mouth curled up, his face and eyes crinkled.

"What?" Smoke asked, knowing with that face his brother

was about to say something funny.

"You can stop looking for more shackles," started Fire.

Smoke winced and said, "I know I am going to regret this…
Why?"

Sparkling eyes returned his stare, and Fire finished, "Seriously you know and I know that this guy is a master magician.
If he wanted shackles anywhere," his eyes darted to the opposite wall, "they would be there!"

Both of them chuckled aloud and Smoke said, "We must be
the first though, our book must be the first to arrive." They
both sort of stared at each other.

"Did you get the feeling that Rhetoric truthfully did not
know why we had arrived with the book?" said Fire in more of
a statement than a question.

Both continued staring at each other sharing the same
thought. They knew who he was, but he had no idea of who
they were or what they could do…that they and the book
were attached. Fire smiled as he watched a whiff of smoke flow
from under his brother's sleeve; and Smoke smiled back into
his red eyes, moving his arms, shaking the chains that held
them, but they did not rattle like normal ones. The sound was
dull and did not clink. "Can you do anything about these,
brother?"

"Looks like metal, but it somehow feels different. It will
take some time," replied Fire. "Time is what we seem to have
a lot of right now. Go for it, turn up the heat!" came back
Smoke, still smiling. Fire did just that, but whatever the chains
were made of was thick and encrusted, or coated with the
dried black mist of Rhetoric himself. The process would be
slow. That was when they both felt it move…

* * *

She was tall and stood straight, hair blackened by the mist, matching the black boots she wore that came just above her knees, and were tied with a single strand of black leather. The garment upon her body hung loosely barely covering the black green stripes that covered her arms, legs and torso, then continuing up the left side of her face...a "gift" from her father when she had betrayed him with Rhetoric. She would never be confused with her goody two shoes sister, Ciera. She had caught them both with help from Enol the knight would be magician, and their mutual parent, Quinn. Her face held a half smile as her eyes crinkled and her wings flared showing vivid blues and green, the original colors of her youth that still remained, and the clipped portion that prevented flight... another "gift" from her father. She thought to herself, "You will get yours, my dear sister; I promised then and I promise now."

Anya, daughter of Quinn and Saviera and sister to Ciera, stood along side Rhetoric looking down at the massive table they stood in front of, as mist poured from his mouth onto it. A puddle formed and he passed a striped hand over it, causing the surface to glaze over. "Where are they now my love?" asked Anya. Rhetoric glanced over at her, his lips pinched; his eyes mere black disks in their sockets, then back towards the puddle. "I have almost located Anhur..."

CHAPTER VII

The Forest of Fire

DAY LOOKED around and back at the other faeries noticing their weary but alert faces, as they scanned the area around them. The stories of the night before were still vivid in their minds; they were leery of IBNot, and watched their steps as they maneuvered up the rocky trail. She sat on Enol's right shoulder, her wings tired. Her brother, Night; sat further back on the shoulder of Sneakin. As with all faeries with wings flight was possible, but not extended flight. For she and her brother and their size, walking like the rest was not an option. They just could not have kept up and both had welcomed the rest.

Enol gently placed his hand on Ciera's shoulder; she was two steps ahead as usual. "I have not seen Id and Odd all day."

"I sent them to scout ahead this morning," she answered with a quick twist of her head, quickly flipping her eyes at him, then back at the stony trail.

"It is almost noon," she continued; "I am sure we will hear

from them soon."

It was not long and once again Enol touched his wife's shoulder, this time to point ahead of them as they broke the tree line. Ciera looked up and stopped in her tracks, as did the others behind her. All stared at the huge boulder that lay in their path just fifty yards ahead; wedged between two walls of rock that extended what seemed to be forever to the right or left. It was at that very moment, Id and Odd slid up the nearest tree.

"Ciera, Enol!" Id sputtered out. He seemed beyond excited, and babbled the same way, making no sense whatsoever. Ciera turned to Odd, her eyebrow rising in question.

Odd spoke up in his normal gruff and grumpy voice, "What my supposed better half is trying to say my queen is that the boulder may be large, but it shields you from what is on the other side."

"And what is that," her eyes sparkled now with anticipation. She had been bored with the trail for quite awhile now.

Id gave Odd no chance to respond this time, "A soldier…a soldier who carries the shield of Rhetoric!"

Ciera's eyes continued their sparkling as she turned to Enol. "We are close, very close to the Forest of Fire. This soldier," her eyes shot back at the others then down, as she paused. Only Enol saw them squint, just a little, then she finished, "A sentry."

She turned to the others, "Stay here." Then to Id and Odd, "Go, keep watch on the soldier, we will find a way around this boulder…and stay out of sight." She touched her husband's hand, her eyebrow now up and fully cocked. "Let's check it out."

Day flew from Enol to Sneakin's other shoulder, noticing the concern in his eyes and whispered, "I know, Sneak; I'm worried too. We will give them ten minutes." Fifteen sets of eyes never left their backs as they started up the trail toward the boulder. Sneakin simply nodded in agreement.

When they were about forty yards from the others, Enol touched his wife's hand. "This soldier he is not just a sentry, is he?"

Her reply was quick. "No, a sentry of sorts, but he is most likely a soldier of Abedjou…a ghost soldier."

"Ghost soldier?" Enol asked.

Ciera smiled at the way he had said it; and answered, "Yes, probably Anhur, one who brings the distant one…in our case that would be Rhetoric. I have seen him in years past, but have never had the need to engage him. I am also sure; he has seen me. He will be bearded, and in human form; with four feathers braided into his hair, a symbol of courage to his people; defending himself with a lance, spear or possibly bow and arrow."

They had reached the boulder now, and she paused, pointing just to the left side of its base, where it seemed passage might be an option.

Ciera looked back at him, her hand now upon his sleeve. "As a ghost, our weapons are useless against him. The only way to defeat him is with his own weapon, what ever that may be. Follow my lead, just this once, dear. His ancient people were good and peaceful; but the shell of his essence, his ghost; is now controlled by Rhetoric, and he must not be allowed to tell him how far we have come." She turned, not waiting for an answer, and headed toward the left side of the boulder.

Enol followed thinking, "I will this time, but I will be ready."

Ciera turned back briefly, smiling. "Good."

The opening was tight, and both of them had to remove their swords quietly from their sheaths to get through. Just ten feet from the other side of the passage, the back of the soldier could be seen, as he stood looking out over the valley beyond.

Enol glanced over at her thinking, "Anhur?"

"Yes," she sent back silently.

There was no color to him, except for the four yellow feathers that lay down the back of his head, atop the braid of gray hair. He stood absolutely still, only his head showed movement, as it slowly went from side to side searching, waiting for them.

A screech from above caused him to look up. Anhur raised his bow, arrow set, ready to launch at Cedrick. In an instant, Enol's hand was on the hilt of his sword.

Ciera never looked back to know this, but thought, "Wait," as if she had. Then, she stepped into full view of the soldier, Anhur. She spoke loudly, bravely, without hesitation. "Let the hawk fly! It is I you want!" Cold, dark eyes turned her way, causing him to lower his bow, and a sort of smile appeared on the ghost soldier's face.

Ciera continued, "If, it is a fight you want, you will have it. But, I warn you, I will win."

Anhur opened his mouth and a guttural stony voice answered. "You are the hawk, and the hawk is you, without the hawk I will win." He swiftly raised the bow and let the arrow fly toward Cedrick, causing Enol to now pull his sword from its sheath, ready for whatever would come next. He glanced over toward his wife and saw her eyes dancing with excitement, hearing her thought of "I wouldn't do that;" and then aloud to Anhur, "You should not have done that," as she watched the arrow fly from the ghost soldier's bow. Enol followed her stare, and then the arrow as it moved toward its target. Cedrick saw the arrow too, snatching it from the air with his right talons, turning in mid flight, and slinging it with ease, back at the ghost soldier.

This time it met its target, and Anhur fell to his knees looking at Cedrick with shock in his eyes; then towards Ciera as he crumpled down, laid to rest by his own weapon. Black dust rose up now from the ground as it rumbled, and shook all around the ghost soldier, absorbing him back to the place in which he belonged. Only his bow and quiver still holding arrows within it remained, when it settled.

Once again Sneakin visibly made them jump when he spoke up from behind them, holding his fist in the air, yelling, "Go Cedrick!"

"Yes," agreed Enol, picking up the bow and quiver adding, "Very impressive indeed!" Ciera smiled at them both, saying, "Its a little game we have played in the past." She winked at Cedrick, as he flew up landing on a nearby outcropping of rock.

"Oh, if birds could smile," Ciera heard him think.

"Oh, but you do my friend," responded Enol aloud.

Cedrick screeched softly back at him, then turned towards Ciera and screeched softly once more saying, "He understands me."

She responded, "I know."

Everyone else was just behind Sneakin, all making their way through the opening, and around the huge boulder. Peakin, who was one of the first ones through, stepped over to the top of the knoll where Anhur had stood, and looked on the other side.

"Enol, Ciera, Sneakin! Everyone! Come see its beautiful!"

The whole group went to join her, all seeing how right she was. It truly was beautiful. Enol looked away from the beauty ahead, noticing the way his wife was looking at it. Ciera glanced over catching his stare, and said aloud to them all; "Do not let those grassy fields, the smell of jasmine, or fruit covered trees fool you for this is the Land of Not."

She could hear them whispering as she took the small pack from her back.

"What does she mean?" "Land of Not?" "What about the Forest of Fire?"

Ciera opened her bag adding, "This is the land where nothing is as it seems."

More whispers. They watched as their queen pulled from her pack a small driftwood mirror. It seemed to grow in size as it came into view, and Enol reached out to hold one side; remembering it, and how it had helped him many years before. Sneakin grabbed the other side and it grew to almost four feet wide. The driftwood itself, looked dead to the eye, yet moved around the mirror as if it were alive.

Ciera turned them both so as to fill the mirror with the beauty of the Land of Not but that is not what showed. "Behold the Mirror of Mordeau, or the Mirror of Truth! To travelers past, who did not survive our present path, this was known as the Land of Not." Ciera pointed at the mirror. "But, this mirror allows us to see the truth. Behold the Forest of Fire!"

Flames filled the mirror, there seemed no end to them, and in that instant all knew they would have to go through them.

"My queen," spoke up Saynk, his normally smooth watery voice was broken by his need for water. "Is this Mirror of Truth a key?"

"You need water my friend," was her reply, eyes filled with concern, as she looked over at Cinq and Sunck as well.

"A bath would be nice, but we are fine for now," he responded.

Ciera was not convinced, but answered his question. "Yes, the mirror is a key. We may very well need it later, but the laws of magic allow only a single use as you know. We must get through the Forest of Fire, so using it to see the truth of the Land of Not can not be avoided."

There was silence now, as they all watched the flames in the mirror, no path shown through them. Enol spoke first amid the silence stating the obvious. "Even through the mirror no path is visible, we will have to create one." Ciera looked over at him that smile playing upon her lips he was so familiar with. "And what goes through that pretty head now, my dear?" he asked coyly.

She winked and turned her head toward the Amberwood faeries sitting on the tip of the knoll, still staring, mesmerized at the mirror. "Maurie, my dear, please come here."

The young faerie stood, walking toward Ciera. She looked up at her queen; and for the first time Enol saw the wind swirling behind those large light blue eyes and he smiled. Ciera's question was short, "How fast can you run?"

"Fast enough. What is it that you require?" she replied.

"The wind within you," answered Ciera.

Maurie raised her eyebrow looking over at the mirror, and the flames within it. "You want a path."

"Yes."

"Through the flames…"

"Yes."

"How deep are the flames?" Maurie asked.

Ciera gently turned her away from the mirror and her focus on the flames.

"Look beyond, see the open meadows?"

"Yes."

"They are that deep. I figure them to be within the flight of a well released arrow, dear; perhaps five hundred paces."

Ciera, who had been standing at her side during their conversation, now turned to see Maurie's facial expression. The young faerie lowered her eyes, as if in contemplation; then raised her windswept eyes to her queen.

"In the last year I started to feel the need to expel the wind within me, to just blow sort of…a release of pressure, I guess. I do not know how much pressure is truly inside of me."

"What are you trying to say?" Ciera questioned, and innocence answered.

"Can I just put the fire out?"

All that heard her say it, stood motionless and speechless, except of course Ciera, whose one eyebrow was held to its highest point. "Can you do that dear?"

Maurie turned her eyes to the mirror watching the flames, then stared at the Land of Not and its size. "I think so."

Enol touched Ciera's hand and thought, "Let her cut the path. Getting through to Madrena and Rhetoric is the main objective. If she has wind left on the other side, she can blow it out then. We just should not risk the '*I think so*' part." She winked back quickly letting him know she agreed.

"Maran, your father said you were special, and you are." The young faerie smiled up at her. "Your power of wind is new to you however, so let's just take this one step at a time. We need you to blow a path wide enough so all can fit through, for what we think, is just about five hundred paces. That I am sure you can do. After that, if you still have wind; put it out, dear." Her childlike face lit up and the blueness of her eyes that was normally barely visible seemed to light up with more richness of color. Enol took this as a sign and circled his finger in the air to group them together.

"We will have one shot at this," he said. "Stay together. Keep an eye on who's beside you. The heat will be intense, so fold your wings tightly and keep up!"

Ciera put her hand on the Mirror of Mordeau, and it shrank almost immediately, back to original size. Her eyes very seldom left Maurie's eyes, as she watched them get bluer and bluer, and everyone ran toward the flames of the Land of Not. They stopped at the edge, all could feel the radiating heat. Ciera held up the Mirror of Mordeau for all to see just how close they were to the edge of the flames. She looked over to Maurie again, and the small faerie looked back, her eyes now a solid, vibrant moving blue. "Believe in yourself! We believe in you! Are you ready?" There was no hesitation in the young faerie, only the double nod of her head before she turned, once again running towards the flames, and they all followed…because they did believe.

Maurie blew steadily at a fire she could not see, creating a path about thirty feet wide. As the flames extinguished the ground blackened in front of them, sending soot floating upward from the footprints they made. In front of them trees and flowers could be seen, but through the mirror Ciera held high as she followed on Maurie's heels, the others could see the flames on either side of them, not just feel their heat, showing the truth of the Land of Not. Sighs of relief could be heard as two by two their feet touched the grassy meadow on the other side of the Forest of Fire.

Enol's voice immediately boomed out, "Check the person beside you! Sneakin! Head count!" He had barely finished, when a hand from behind touched his arm and pointed back down the blackened path.

"My sister!" warbled Saynk dryly as he crumpled, fainting.

Enol caught him and looked up into Sneakin's eyes who never hesitated, saying, "I will get her!"

He shot forward, wing snapping, in full flight back down the blackened path. Ciera heard the familiar snap of his wing as she pushed the mirror back in her pack and looked up. The Land of Not…the trees, the flowers…all were gone, the reality of the flames now showing through.

She stood immediately yelling, "Stay to the center Sneak!

The heat...your wings!" Her words were too late. A single invisible flame licked at his right wing, burning it at the tip sending a visible puff of smoke into the air. Ciera turned to call Maurie, but the young faerie was already there, running past her down the blackened path, blowing and fanning the flames away from Sneakin and Cinq.

Their eyes met and Maurie yelled; "Shield yourselves!"

The tall faerie lay down, wing still smoking and covered his friend with his own body and wings saying quickly, "Do your thing sweetie!"

...And Maurie did. All watched, amazed at the power of the wind within her. She blew steadily in a wide sweep, away from them, then back across, waving her hand; signaling Sneakin to go. Enol watched as one of his bravest faeries scooped up the dry and cracking body of Cinq. He yelled for Night and Day, "Fly up! Find water!" then glanced down at Saynk and over to Sunck, cracks in their faces starting even as he added to the others, "Leave your canteens! Find water!"

Ciera, now cradling Sunck, looked up at Enol, tears and anger in her eyes, then back down at the two withering faeries. "Hang in there you two, we will find water!" Gently, she placed Sunck at her husband's feet. She stood, watching as Piggett, Skinny and Hyde took off across the meadow, while Tarin and the other three Amberwood faeries took off in the other direction, in search of the precious life giving water their friends so desperately needed. Sneakin laid Cinq down gently on the ground next to her brother, and he and Ciera dropped their canteens and took off.

Maurie touched Enol's shoulder. "How can I help?"

He looked up at her. She did not look tired nor spent in any way. He glanced over her shoulder at the Forest of Fire that was no more. She had blown it out in its entirety.

Enol cupped her small face, "Are you okay?"

"Yeah, I'm fine," she answered, without hesitation.

He smiled briefly at her, glancing once more at the deceased Forest of Fire. "Ok, use the canteens, pour the water over them. Just a little at a time…like this." Enol poured the water carefully making sure every drop landed on them; they must not waste any.

Together they watched, as the parched bodies seemed to soak up every drop. Slowly and carefully, they drizzled the water carefully down their friends' arms and legs, on their bodies, and gently patted their faces with wet hands. The canteens of water emptied one by one until just two were left. Sunck was the first to speak, and you could tell it was hard for him to do. "My sister, my brother…"

"Everyone is out looking for water," answered Enol, as he looked over at Saynk and saw him move, but Cinq still showed no signs of life.

He turned back to Sunck. "They are fine, and you will be too, just relax. Let the water replenish you." The cracked, parched faerie closed his eyes half dreaming of their private pool at home, and half thinking of the concern he had most certainly seen in Enol's eyes as he had looked at his brother and sister. He drifted off.

Enol turned to Maurie, "You work on these two. I need to concentrate on Cinq." She nodded, glancing over at the still, ashen colored water fairy then turned to Enol. He saw the concern in her eyes; and he placed his finger over his mouth, darting his eyes over to Sunck and Saynk and she understood. Slowly and gently, Enol patted water over the body of Cinq, all the while noticing the cracks in her skin. They were deep, much deeper than Saynk's or Sunck's…much. The heat of the fire had literally evaporated what little moisture all three had upon entering the path through the Forest of Fire. Cinq's extended stay had drawn even more from her.

What seemed like hours, but was actually only minutes, passed before the others returned triumphant in their search. Water was not far away. Sneakin ran immediately over to Enol when they landed, eyes filling with tears, as he looked down at Cinq.

"No! It cannot be," he mumbled, then louder, "The water! That is all she needs. I will take her to the water now!" He scooped up the seemingly lifeless and frail body flying up towards the pond they had found, the glimmer of tears still in his eyes.

No one said a word as Enol picked up Saynk, and Peakin and Ciera each took one of Sunck's shoulders. The two were drained but seemed to be coming around. They had to get them to the water.

"It's not far," said Tarin to Enol in almost a whisper, adding, "Just beyond the first set of trees."

There it was as they broke through the trees, a pond so big that the three water faeries had they been at their best, would have played in for hours. Sneakin stood waist deep cradling Cinq, her still dry body floating easily on the water, as he gently pushed more of the life giving liquid over her, but still she did not come around.

Enol, Ciera, and Peakin carried Saynk and Sunck into the water beside him dousing them as well. Eyes met, and Sneakin shook his head, tears once again welling up in the eyes of the tallest and bravest faerie of them all.

A dry cracked voice then spoke. It was Sunck. "How are Cinq and Saynk?"

Ciera tousled his hair gently. "Saynk is coming around like you. Cinq is not moving yet."

"We must take her," he warbled back, looking over at his sister, then to his brother who opened his eyes briefly and nodded in agreement.

"Take her where?" asked Sneakin.

"To the bottom," answered Sunck as he struggled to stand in the water, and with the help of Ciera did.

"You are still too weak."

"Yes, but the water at the bottom is better…more pressure. It will help us all."

Saynk now stood as well, legs shaking, with the help of Enol. "You must move on," he said simply, his voice straining.

The brothers clasped their hands together supporting each other, and moved slowly toward Cinq adding, "We will catch up." Gently they took their sister from Sneakin, their eyes meeting his, saying, "Thank you friend."

Slowly they moved, holding her arms as her seemingly lifeless body hung between them, moving deeper into the water. Sunck looked up at Enol and Ciera as Saynk continued to push water up, and over the body of his dry and cracked sister. "Push on! We will find you!" he rasped and under the water they went as all the others stood silent watching their friends disappear into the depths of the pond.

Enol was the first to speak. His eyes still stared at the spot where they had gone under.

"They are right. We must move on." He took Ciera's hand wrapping it between his, both still standing in the water waist deep.

"I do not like leaving them," she answered.

"Neither do I, but we must."

Peakin looked over to her brother, who now stood rigid still looking down at where Cinq and her brothers had went down. "Cinq told me once you were the bravest faerie she had ever seen."

"But yet, I could not save her," he answered slowly.

Enol placed a hand on his shoulder. "We do not know that

my friend. You did all you could. I do believe there is a chance for Cinq, and that is because of you." He looked at Sneakin's burned wing. "Let's take care of that wing."

Slowly they all moved out of the water, every one of them glancing back at least once to the spot their friends had disappeared.

It was Night who took their attention away from the three water faeries when he spoke up from atop a rock at the shoreline. "Has anyone seen Piggett, Skinny, and Hyde?" as he turned scanning the tree line.

Ciera stood, dripping at the waters edge, "They crossed the meadow by the Forest of Fire in search of water."

"Rest here, my queen. We will return there and bring them," responded Tarin automatically as he and his small band took off, not waiting for an answer.

Ciera agreed with a silent nod as she took one last look towards the center of the pond then spread her wings, something she had not done that day. It felt good. She shot herself upward, spiraling as she did, slinging the water away from her. Peakin and Sneakin followed.

Enol, however, stood on the ground trying to squeeze the water from his shirt yelling up, "Not fair!"

Ciera laughed from up above then flew down, landing next to Maurie who had stayed behind and whispered in her ear.

The small Amberwood faerie stepped up to him and said, "Just turn slowly."

Enol's eyebrows shot up and he glanced to Ciera then back to Maurie, "Easy does it though, okay?" he said; his voice a little shaky, as he saw the wind moving in those eyes and remembered the power of it.

"No worries. I can control it my friend." Slowly, he turned completely around just once, as the wind within her blew every drop of the water from his face, body and clothes. Enol placed a dry hand on Maurie's blond head, "Thank you my dear."

She barely had time to nod a 'no problem' when Tarin's voice could be heard as he and his group approached without smiles. "We could not find them Enol. We searched the meadow and beyond." He held up three swords. "Except for these, there is no sign of them." His eyes went from the Enol to the swords then back at Enol. "Are these theirs?" he asked. His eyes were filling with concern. He looked from Maurie and the other Amberwood faeries, then to Ciera who was now at his side, examining the swords.

"Could this IBNot you have told us about, my queen; have gotten to them?" asked Tarin. Her eyes scanned the tree line behind him. "IBNot, himself; is a spy not a fighter. Rhetoric would have to be working through him for that."

She paused, thinking to herself allowing only Enol to hear, not wanting to alarm the others. "It was like they just disappeared, why else would their swords be left behind?"

"Or faded, like the books," he shot back.

Her eyes narrowed and she asked aloud to Tarin, "Did you leave a sign, letting them know where we are?"

The reply came swiftly, "Yes, my queen."

Ciera nodded and smiled, letting him see her appreciation of his fore thought, "Good thinking, please leave another sign here." Her eyes lowered to the swords once more, her thoughts filled with concern for the three faeries. Sneakin and Peakin stepped up to Tarin and he nodded as they said, "Allow us to hold those for you." Each slid one easily into their sheaths along with their own sword, with Sneakin tucking the third in the strap that held his dagger.

Enol's face, as well, was filled with concern for the three missing faeries, as he placed his hand on Ciera's, "This is not like them," he thought.

"I know," she returned; and then aloud to the others said, "We must continue on, Piggett, Skinny and Hyde will catch up." The nine remaining faeries nodded in agreement, even Cedrick screeched from above, although all were unconvinced of their friends' safety. Both Ciera and Enol heard their thoughts but were silent. In just less than two hours, they had become six less.

Silence continued as Sneakin's singed wing was tended to by Bramer, the medicine man of the Amberwood faeries, while Tarin and the other two left the sign. Still silent, they moved on towards the fortress of Rhetoric, each glancing back often until the pond was completely out of sight.

* * *

Rhetoric sat staring into the puddle. Why could he not locate Anhur? There could only be one answer…he had met his fate, and most likely with the help of Ciera and Enol.

If that was true, they were nearing the Forest of Fire or possibly just past it. His lips curled in anticipation of the damage it would, or could have done. A strand of mist seeped from the corner of his mouth.

He snapped his head around looking for Anya, shouting her name, forgetting he had sent her to check on the ravens. They should be here very soon, hopefully with the trunk and the thirteenth book. He called again for her, and this time she answered from the hallway across the room.

Rhetoric watched as Anya walked toward him. She had been beautiful once, but now the stripes that covered her body pitted her smooth skin of yesteryear. The mist had not reacted with her body as it had with his. It did not move for her, instead it had rotted her teeth and gnarled her hair.

She spoke, "There is no sign of them on the far horizon yet. It should not be long; I will wait for them." Anya turned to go, noticing Rhetoric's eyes upon her and the way they were looking and she turned back towards him. At first their association had been one of mutual attraction, both attracted to the want and desire for power each craved, but now it was one more of need. They were meant to rule…*she* was meant to rule and she, Anya, would do just about anything to make sure that happened. Was he telling her everything, she wondered?

"How many books have arrived?"

His eyes glanced towards the hallway that led to the turret rooms. "At last count, one. We should maybe check it out though, seems they come with faeries attached."

Anya knitted her brows which had gnarled as well, giving her facial features a bizarre twist. "Faeries?" she asked.

"Yes," he answered, "Somehow they must be linked to the book, for it and they appear together."

Anya looked down at the mist that trailed from him. There were two trails of it leading back towards the turret rooms now.

"So you have captured them. The mist…it holds them?"

"Yes, but there will be more as the books arrive I think." Rhetoric paused, standing. "I will need your assistance," he paused again, now looking straight at her, knowing her vicious side. "Not one faerie must be harmed for now, Anya, not one."

"You are asking a lot." She said it snidely, with a small curl in the corner of her mouth. Rhetoric did not smile back, "Not one Anya. I must know how they are bound to the book. Once I control the books; I hope to control the faeries as well."

Anya's eyes squinted at him, "I or we?"

Rhetoric saw her anger rising, he must appease her for now. "Of course we," he replied smiling back at her, though not wanting to. She was very skillful with her sword; he would need her. He waved at the hallway, "Shall we?"

Anya gave him a slight nod and stepped toward the hallway. She would have to watch him. Of this she was sure, she felt it.

CHAPTER VIII

Unexpected Allies

THEY HAD made good time since leaving the pond, and their sick friends and Piggett, Skinny and Hyde. The rolling meadows they now traveled on wove their way through two forests and was covered in wonderfully soft grass. Ciera was well ahead of the others, loving the feel of it beneath her feet, as opposed to the stony trails they had been on. She topped a small hill, seeing on her left beautiful stands of daisies that bordered the dark forest on that side and for the first time she let her worried thoughts of Madrena mellow. For just one moment she allowed herself to breath in the beauty around her, closing her eyes to appreciate it even more.

However, with that breath, her nose immediately crinkled. A smell, musty…almost sweet, suddenly filled the air. "What's that?" tumbled from her mouth, her eyes opening instantly. She turned to the right, saw nothing, and took two more steps down the hill. "Mmmh…" She did not smell it in that direction. Was it just something riding on the wind, and now gone?

She doubted it. A few more steps down the incline, Ciera turned back to the left and her eyes widened. The source of the smell was discovered. Only two words left her mouth, "Oh my!"

Two elk, larger than she had ever seen, stood very close, almost too close. How had she not seen them? Had she been so absorbed in the flowers and beauty of this place? They must have come from the forest when her eyes were closed. She stood quiet, she was not afraid...*she was in awe.* They were beautiful massive animals, one male, one female. She watched as the female lay down upon the soft grass and breathed heavily, as if thoroughly exhausted. The male lowered his huge head towards her, pushing air quickly from his nostrils, as if asking her if she was okay, and she answered by lowering her head to the grass.

Ciera moved her hand slowly across her chest to the hilt of the sword, contemplating on pulling it. The male stirred, raising his mighty rack, making his size even more incredible. He stared straight at her, she at him, their eyes locked. There was no time to move, no time to think, the elk was upon her almost instantly, her sword still in its sheath.

He pushed her up and around his snout, as if she were an extension of his own body, tucking her under his chin; then bringing her to the ground, placing his mighty hoof on Ciera's back, holding her there securely.

His snout stayed just above her head. She could hear his breathing, feel it pulsating through his hoof, blowing the tendrils of dangling hair downwards around her face. She waited. The breathing stopped suddenly as the great elk looked up towards the hill she had just come down. Ciera stretched her neck, looking too. Her comrades were just topping the hill and Enol was pulling his sword! One arm had landed outstretched towards the hillside and she waved her hand signaling them to stay where they were, telling Enol by thought, that she was fine.

"We stand ready!" he shot back, lips never moving.

Ciera smiled briefly, responding, "You're gettin' good, husband!"

His "I'll bet your eyes are sparkling!" answer made her half grin appear.

Immediately the snout was down upon her again, and the mighty hoof pressed a little harder. The huge elk cocked his head slightly and thundered, "You are either very brave, or very stupid. What is your name?"

"Ciera, Queen of all faeries," she stated firmly.

He glared at her deeply, saying, "Then you are brave... mmm." The hoof on her back eased off, but remained just inches away. There was silence then more thunder. "So Ciera, Queen of all faeries did you come to fight?"

"No sir," she turned her head and body slowly to face him, so as to look directly in his eyes. "In my land fighting is the last option. I would rather be your friend first, not your enemy."

The male elk once again raised his snout, tossing it towards Enol and the others, his hoof still just above her. "And them... what do they believe?" he asked in a lower but still thunderous voice.

"As I do, they stand behind me in all ways, mighty one." Ciera could feel his stare now even more; searching, searching for truthfulness in her eyes.

She continued, "With that said however, I cannot promise what will happen next, or how they will react," her head nodded towards the hill, "If we cannot be friends."

The massive animal gazed back at his female companion, who stared back at him waiting for a sign, then back to Ciera. Slowly, he moved his massive hoof, stepping back away from her as he did. From atop the hill, Enol let out a sigh of relief as his wife stood and faced the enormous elk.

"A fresh beginning then," she said bowing, "It is a pleasure to meet you. My name is Ciera and yours?"

"I am Logren, Leader of the Herd...or what is left of it," he replied, glancing back at the tree line behind the female elk then continued. "My wife, Maleah and I have just come from across the Barren. The rest of my herd is close behind us."

Ciera followed Logren's gaze towards the dark forest. "And this Barren you speak of, it is just beyond the tree line?" she asked. Enol and the others approached before the mighty elk could answer. "Logren, this is my husband, Enol."

"You have a very brave wife, sir," the elk responded.

"Yes, so brave she scares me sometimes!" Enol answered, arching his eyebrow.

"I know what you mean," answered Logren nodding toward his own wife.

Ciera smiled towards Maleah with a nod then turned back towards the mighty elk.

"Tell me more of this Barren. What's on the other side?"

"The Barren has existed since I can remember. It surrounded what was our home. Over the last few years we noticed that either our land was shrinking, or the Barren was growing." He paused again, looking back toward the tree line once more.

"I would venture to say that the Barren was growing," broke in Enol. "More evidence that Rhetoric's evil is at work."

Logren's eyes flashed towards him instantly, "Rhetoric?"

"Your eyes, and the way you say his name suggest you know him," Enol answered.

"He steals our young, enslaving them....an evil magician, out for his own good. One thing we do not know, however; is where he lives."

Ciera touched the beard of hair that hung from his chin,

tugging it gently making him turn toward her. "We do."

The corners of the mighty elks mouth curled up, his eyes narrowed. "And what is your destiny with Rhetoric, Ciera Queen of the Faeries?" he said, staring straight at her for just a second, then glancing back at the tree line once more.

Enol noticed the setting sun. "Logren, it is obvious you care about the rest of your herd the way you keep eyeing that tree line. Let us make camp; we will wait for the rest of your herd with you and talk. I have a feeling we can be of great help to each other."

Logren looked to Enol nodding while his eyes showed anticipation for what they had to tell him, "Agreed."

The mighty elk then lowered his stare, turning toward his wife, and Ciera watched as he stopped at her side, turning back towards her. "One question if I may." He glanced quickly up to her eyes, then back to her waist. "Is that a dragonfly dagger?"

"Yes," Ciera responded simply, as her own mouth curled upward.

"Then could it be that a magician will be losing his life soon?" Logren continued. "That's two questions," Ciera laughed, but Logren just smiled and continued.

"Stories have been told of such a dagger."

She smiled back at him, eyebrow raised, interrupting. "Later, my new friend; all your questions will be answered. We must make camp and rest for a short time."

The huge elk nodded, his eyes moving from the dagger to Ciera's eyes then he turned to stand vigil for the other members of his herd.

Ciera watched him as he stepped away, thinking, "What a massive creature to move with such majestic grace. Seems we may have a common goal…that of rescuing our children." She continued to watch as Logren lay down next to his wife,

Maleah, his eyes never leaving the tree line. Ciera had seen pain in her eyes, perhaps their child had been taken as well.

Enol stepped up behind her, placing his hands on her shoulders. "I heard that and I think you are right."

"What? Are you reading my thoughts now, without me knowing it?" She twirled around to face him, a smile on her face.

"Well not really, I just hear you think." He was almost blushing. "I don't hear anyone else like that, only you."

She smiled, pecking him on the lips, saying with a wink, "Well, this was not one of the side effects listed in the recipe to transfer years."

Up went that eyebrow of his, "Side effects? Did you say side effects? What side effects *were* listed?"

She was laughing now, and he joined in, slipping her hand into his.

"Let's find a good place for the tent dear," Ciera said. She was still laughing and with all that had happened, it felt good.

* * *

The sun had just broken the horizon and rays shot forth lighting up the area. Enol stood silent allowing the others to sleep, having his morning coffee. Three more elk had arrived during the night, and slept near the opposite tree line. He stooped over picking up the pot, and poured another cup. The talk with Logren had gone well last night. Unfortunately, his son had indeed been one of the children taken; he was all too eager to help in the destruction of Rhetoric and IBNot. Ciera had explained to him and Maleah, that it was most likely IBNot who had done the actual stealing of their young, while performing Rhetoric's bidding. He recalled the angry look that had come over Logren's face, and what his immediate thought had been. "I would not want to be in the path of those antlers." He smiled in remembrance of the moment.

Enol's head snapped left. What was that? He had heard it earlier too, as he was making his coffee. Once be warned he thought silently. Twice be aware, as his knight training days reminded him. His eyes probed the tree line just ten or so feet from the other side of their tent…nothing.

"Enol!" There! There it was again. Three times, take action! Someone or something had said his name. He was sure of it. It had been no more than a whisper, but he had heard it. Pulling his sword, he once again searched the tree line for any movement and saw none.

It came again. "Enol!" Slowly he walked toward the first trees, trying to see in the darkness of the thicker trees beyond where the voice had called from, he was sure. The grass underfoot was wet, so his footsteps made no sound; no matter, he was sure whoever was calling his name could see him already.

He had just passed the first tree when… "AAAHHH! AAAHHH!" Enol just about jump out of his skin! He swung his sword instantly, ready to fight.

"It's just us Enol!" Id and Odd were panting. "We were sleeping! You scared us nearly to death!"

"Death is right! You startled me as well!" Enol yelled back. He had stopped the sword just inches from the tree, and now dropped it back into its sheath. "Did you guys call my name?"

Odd answered, grumpy as usual, "And what part of *we were sleeping* did you not understand?"

Enol squinted at him. "I, only just started my second cup of coffee Odd. It's too early for sarcasm. However, if you guys did not call my name, who did? …and they did, four times." His eyes searched the forest as far as the light would allow him, no movement. "The morning before we arrived at the Forest of Fire you felt something too, when you were alone my husband, and now that something is calling your name? I think we should start thinking of you as a wanted commodity. Someone or something out there wants you."

Enol turned around to find his wife. "You are thinking IBNot?"

Ciera spoke more firmly now. "Absolutely, it makes perfect sense. Only a magician can rid the world of another magician, why wouldn't Rhetoric send him. Through IBNot Rhetoric lives, through IBNot, Rhetoric could kill you and power over the books could be his."

Enol gazed into her eyes, the half smile coming into view slowly as he walked toward her. "You do have a way of sneaking up behind me." He kissed her. "Good morning beautiful. I promise I will be careful."

"Do not doubt Rhetoric's abilities. You must stay close to me." She was speaking firmly again, her own half smile smiling back, her left hand on the dragonfly dagger.

"That's not a problem," he responded immediately, pulling her even closer.

Suddenly the moment was broken by loud snoring, Id and Odd must have fallen back to sleep. Ciera started to laugh, but stopped saying, "Wait, is that snoring or scratching?" Together they walked back to the tree just a few yards away where Enol had first found them.

"Id, Odd are you still here?" he asked.

A grumble, an AAHEM, and finally Id's voice could be heard, but not from the tree just in front of them.

"Yes Ciera!" he answered.

She stepped lightly around the tree playfully, thinking they were toying with her, Enol followed, but the faces were not there, only a message scrawled on the tree by either knife, or claw.

Have you checked your books lately?

Their eyes met briefly as Ciera grabbed his hand, placed it on her forehead and closed her eyes. Instantly they were in the mighty oak, their home, standing directly in front of the shelves. There were only two books remaining...Sneakin and Peakin's and Cinq, Saynk and Sunck's.

Enol turned, scanning the library. "Where is everyone?"

She did not answer, but walked to the window, pulling him with her and together they saw the bodies of the soldier faeries outside.

Ciera was the first to speak, her face now ashen at the sight of their friends.

"I do not see Fire and Smoke or any of the other faeries attached to the books for that matter." Enol turned from the window and stared at the empty shelves with an almost stunned look.

"Maybe, they were so attached to their book," he paused; his eyes getting suddenly bigger as he looked at the last two books remaining. "We have to go back...NOW!"

It was then that Ciera turned her eyes away from the soldiers outside and saw the titles on those books and the dirt going up the stairs.

"You go. I will be right there!" She let go of his hand and ran up to Madrena's room as Enol disappeared back to the tree. Her fears were confirmed, the dirt trail led directly to where she had left her daughter's crown. It was gone.

She closed her eyes, and was instantly at the tree in front of the scrawled message. Whatever or whoever had scratched that message was unimportant right now, although they could pretty much bet it was IBNot, once more acting on behalf of Rhetoric; his way of rubbing the books and the possession of them in their faces.

Enol was already running towards the group of tents, stopping in front of Night and Day's, which was set just at eye level on a thick bough of an elm tree. He did not wait to announce his presence, but flung open the small tent flap in almost a rage.

"Night! Day! Are you here?" No answer and no one. Only their swords and daggers, that lay on their bedding, showed they were ever there.

"Their book was not on the shelf," he said quickly, noticing Ciera running towards him. "Nor Piggett, Skinny and Hyde's," she added. Their eyes met briefly; then slowly both turned, staring at the tent of Sneakin and Peakin. Both rushed towards it. Something was moving inside.

"Sneak! Peakin!" He flung open their flap.

"What's all the commotion about Enol? Is something wrong? Did something happen?" Peakin asked. She stood in the doorway and her eyes squinted up at him, as the morning sun snuck through the fingers she held up to shade them.

"Not yet thank goodness! Please get ready to go. We will talk while we walk."

Peakin nodded, ducking back into the tent to rouse her brother.

Enol turned and together he and Ciera broke down their own tent, all the while wondering how they could keep Sneakin and Peakin safe from Rhetoric. His thoughts turned to the second book on the shelf, the book of Cinq, Saynk, and Sunck. Maybe they should send Cedrick back to check on them. A loud screech was heard from above instantly, and Enol watched as the great hawk flew back toward the pond without hesitation. He glanced over at Ciera who was rousing Tarin and his group. If they flanked either side, keeping Sneakin and Peakin in the center of the group with Ciera and him, all eyes would be upon them, watching them. Rhetoric had been busy, ten books in three days.

The bag was packed. They were ready to go. Together Enol and Ciera walked to the center of the meadow and he started to speak but she stopped him placing a finger on his lips. "I agree. I told Tarin and his group to split up, two and two, hugging the tree lines, with Maurie in the middle with us. There is one more thing," she paused, lowering her eyes then raising them, concern showing in them, speaking in thought, "I have made a mistake. I left Madrena's crown on her pillow."

"What crown?" he asked.

"The crown that accompanies the thirteenth book, the crown meant for our daughter to wear. Something inside me told me she would return home for some reason and I left it. There was dirt leading up to her room, up the stairs, and on her pillow where I placed it. Rhetoric or his soldiers must have found it, and have returned with it."

"Why would they have felt the need to take it with them?"

Ciera's eyes filled with tears now. "Because of the thirteen emeralds that are embedded in it…we must assume they put two and two together. Rhetoric will know it is Madrena, that she is the thirteenth book." A single tear ran down her cheek, and she added, "I have put our daughter in danger."

Enol took her in his arms, "You yourself said that Madrena will be fine. The crown itself gives her no additional power, does it?

"No," she answered simply, but something inside her wondered.

"Then she will be fine. Somehow, I know that Rhetoric does not have her, that she is even now on her way to us, as we are to her."

Ciera pulled slightly away from him wiping her eyes. "But, he will be looking for her now."

He held her by the shoulders, "What is done cannot be undone. Rhetoric has a lot on his plate right now, what with twenty three more mouths to feed, and us less than a day away. We must continue towards Rhetoric and believe in the power of the books, especially the thirteenth one, yes?" He smiled now and she smiled back.

"Yes my darling." Enol gave her another quick hug and they turned toward their new comrades sharing a last thought.

"It was IBNot who scrawled the message, my husband. Rhetoric wants us to know he has the books."

Enol looked over to her. "Yes, and the faeries attached to them."

Together they walked towards their new comrades hand in hand, to fill them in on what had just happened, and was still happening.

CHAPTER IX

Knowledge is Power

MADRENA SAT perched, feet tucked underneath her, enjoying the last few moments of perfect safety here in Quiviera. Her gaze fell upon the low branches of the nearby bushes and she remembered her first venture into the woods with her mother, her hero, and how she had been afraid.

Mom had made her sit, for an entire day, watching how the shadows and the sun's rays could change your perception of what was really there. How one single ray of sunshine hitting in one spot, at one precise moment, could create a monster and a few moments later could show the leaves that really hung there, creating the illusion. How close branches became shapes of faces resembling bears, or squatting cats, ready to pounce in the shadows of the coming evening; yet showed their beauty and grace in the morning light. Her mother had somehow sensed that fear, and made her face it in future visits to the wild.

This would be her biggest test yet, but grandfather had told her things…things about the magic and powers she had always known she possessed. Her mind became a mixture of the things she had been taught in the last three days and how she longed to see her parents. A twig snapped behind her, making her jump. She turned to find her grandfather and Adren standing there with smiles on their faces, and she returned the same.

"Your ears must have been burning. I was just thinking of you both." Madrena stood up, facing Quinn, giving his almost transparent body a hug.

"You were thinking more of your parents, however," he said; squeezing her shoulders and added, "You can, you know…see them."

She leaned back her head, cocking it ever so slightly, eyebrows raised like her parents. "Even from inside the book? From here?"

"Yes my dear, even from here." He continued, raising a pointed finger to the sky, then to the ground, then to her head, "Because here is here."

"You, grandfather, you will come too!" She changed the subject just as her mother could when her mind was set on something.

"Madrena, did you understand what I meant?" he asked. She did not answer and Quinn frowned. She could think of nothing else but seeing her parents.

"And you, you will come too?" he heard his granddaughter ask Adren.

Adren had seen the brief grimace on Quinn's face. He wondered about it as he turned to Madrena. "Yes, I will come but where?"

There was a sparkle in her eyes when she answered, "To see my parents!" Adren looked to Quinn, wondering if this was the reason for his grimace.

"Yes, and we must listen to what is said," broke in Quinn, his face still serious but the frown was gone. "We need to know how close to Rhetoric's they are."

Madrena winked over at him, "Absolutely!" and walked between them, taking both of their hands, thinking of her mother and father. Instantly they stood in the center of a large, grassy meadow that stretched behind and in front of them, creating a wide path between two tree lines. At the farther tree line, three immense elk lay sleeping, enjoying the coolness of the morning air.

"They're huge!" exclaimed Adren.

Quinn agreed as a frown formed on his face once more, and Madrena noticed this one.

"What grandfather?"

"I have heard of these elk, but they are out of place," he answered, pausing in thought. "What do you mean?" Adren asked.

"I know this…" his finger raised and he moved it back and forth, as if tapping on air, trying to remember. The frown left his face as he did. "I would not be surprised if they are the last of their kind. I once heard they lived in the center of a vast wasteland, measuring miles across on a large oasis; led there by the first magicians themselves, to save them and their kind, safe from the world, safe from harm."

"So why would they have left?"

"Exactly, young man, exactly." Quinn's answer came back quick to Adren.

"Look!" blurted Madrena, "Just beyond the biggest elk."

Ciera and Enol came into view as they topped a small hill, walking directly over to the elk. The three watched as the mightiest of the elk stood, towering over them both. He nodded. The female elk that lay close by seemed to greet them as well. A small glance was shared between the three, all silently agreed that Ciera and Enol must already know them.

"We must move closer to hear," said Madrena stepping forward. She shot a smile back at them, "Hold on! I wouldn't want to lose one of you! I have a feeling this is something none of us wants to miss!" They crossed the meadow quickly and stood within earshot of the group.

Enol could be heard saying, "Logren, Maleah, as you have hopes of saving your son from Rhetoric, we too have faith in saving our daughter from him as well, but we are slowly losing more and more of our friends. We have discovered just this morning that the books we told you about are being stolen by him, and the faeries attached to each are disappearing too."

Madrena's lips pressed together, listening; continuing to watch as her father looked back toward Sneakin and Peakin, nodding at them.

"Their book; along with one other, are the only ones left," he nodded once more toward the two warrior faeries, "They must be protected. If we can hold on to them possibly we will hold on to the last of the books." He paused just ever so briefly, "…and the books must be saved. All we know and love would be in danger if Rhetoric gains complete control over the books."

The huge elk nodded in understanding, but his expression changed as he glanced back over his shoulder, then once again back at Enol and Ciera. "How can we help?" he asked.

Before Enol could answer however, the huge elk once again turned to look, this time turning his entire body to look directly towards Madrena, Quinn and Adren.

"It is said that animals have an incredible sense of smell and can detect even the unseen," spoke up Quinn.

"Well, he most definitely senses us," added Adren.

They watched as Ciera stepped toward the elk, placing her hand on his side.

"What is it, Logren; what do you see?"

His voice rumbled an answer, "Nothing, yet something." His gaze never left Madrena. It was for sure, that he sensed her and the others.

From behind them, the chattering voices of five small faeries could be heard as they crossed the meadow in the direction of Enol, Ciera and the others. Their chattering continued as they walked right through the projected images of Adren, Madrena and Quinn. Only one turned to stare back at the place in which they stood, one who had incredible big blue eyes. The small faerie opened her mouth and blew, as if blowing a willow the wisp into the breeze but what came from her mouth was a gust of wind that blasted right through them and they felt it.

"Wow!" exclaimed Madrena. "Did you two feel that? She is packing some power inside her!"

Quinn answered, "It seems your parents have made some valuable friends in their travels to Rhetoric's fortress."

Adren squeezed Madrena's hand, "Besides the elk, I think I have counted nine in their group now. Not very many to battle Rhetoric, and from what I have heard of him...," he paused, glancing towards Quinn. "Maybe I should come help them. Madrena could stay with you."

He was immediately cut off by Quinn, "I saw this fight for the books years ago, Adren," his eyes softened and he nodded toward his granddaughter. "It is not I that needs to be at her side, but you."

Madrena heard the conversation between them, but concentrated instead on the mighty elk, the one that could sense them, even now his eyes had never left her. Maybe she could use this. She closed her eyes briefly and then announced, "We're going back now." ...And back in Quiviera they were, back in the clearing where they had both found her, before either man could object.

Madrena turned quickly, saying, "Grandfather, Adren and I must go."

Quinn placed a hand on her arm, "I know, for the books, yes?"

She smiled that half smile of her parents, "Yes, but," Her expression changed now to a more serious one. "How do we return to the book and the cave?"

His eyes softened again as he looked at his beautiful grand-daughter, her purple red hair, and how the shorter strands moved lightly around her face on the small breeze, now filling the clearing.

"The thirteenth book was intended for you my dear, created for you long before even I was born, handed down by Adren's ancestors, then given to your mother till the day you would open it. Now that you have, it is always with you."

He smiled squeezing her arm gently, adding, "Remember?" Quinn took her hand holding it in the air, swirling it gently, then made her point at her own head. "Here is here. The book is here."

Her hand went to her throat, seeing in her minds eye the emerald green necklace that she had noticed her mother wearing in the clearing. She felt her grandfather's hand once more on her arm and looked up into his eyes.

"You have opened the book, it is part of you. There is no need for the necklace to hide it," Quinn paused, his mouth curling upward in a playful way, "Here."

He took both her arms, making her hold them out in front of her. "Now think, think of the book, your book…call for it if you feel you must have it in front of you."

She barely had an image of the book, the words on its cover and its parchment pages in her thoughts, when it appeared in her arms. "Well that was pretty neat!" she said, looking up toward Adren whose smile seemed to go from ear to ear.

"Yes it was, my sweet."

Quinn smiled in satisfaction at their astonishment when the book appeared in her arms. "As it was always meant to be, it is part of you. Unlike Night and Day and the other faeries your father was able to attach to the other twelve books, the book and you are one." The elderly magician paused, turning to look out over the clearing towards his home, his transparent body allowing them to see it as well, and he continued.

"Your book, my dear; controls all others. It is the master copy, the original. A book, once again handed down thru time by your people, Adren. For they too, saw this coming of evil and they saw each of you, and they believed."

His eyes seemed to glow a brighter blue than normal as he spoke, the grip of his hand on his staff becoming tighter. "Handed down with the belief that it would one day be powerful enough, through you my dear, to battle evil for possession of the Trunk of Life…and it is."

Madrena looked from her grandfather to Adren, her eyes now alive with anticipation of what was to come. "So that is why the book asked for you first! You truly were destined to be here, to carry me from my home, and keep me safe."

"Yes, you are my destiny." He bowed slightly, but not his head. He winked at her instead, adding, "A destiny I do not regret whatsoever."

Quinn smiled from behind them, as he saw the flinch of Madrena's left eye and the smile she returned to Adren, one of trust and love to come, as he saw it. "Mmm! I did not foresee this part!"

Madrena turned just then catching him smiling, and winked as she shot back, "I heard that!" in thought.

Her face then turned somber as her thoughts returned to what had been said about the missing books and faeries in the clearing. "What is happening to the faeries of the books Rhetoric has already taken, grandfather?" Madrena asked.

Quinn pushed out his lower lip, setting his jaw, then said in a lower than normal voice. "Rhetoric wishes only to control the powers of the books. He cares nothing for those faeries."

Her grandfather placed his hands softly on her shoulders, wiping a tear just falling from the corner of her right eye. "We must focus on what needs to be done first. Get the two remaining books. Rhetoric is a man of evil intentions, he will not do away with something or someone that could be useful in his attempt to control the books, most of all, your book. I feel he will not harm them until he is sure they are of no use to him"

A small smile formed as she wiped a tear from her other eye. "That is not going to happen, grandfather." Madrena placed the book on the grass, lifting its cover and flipped the pages. She did not see her grandfather as he thrust his hand toward Adren, gripping his lower arm just below the elbow, causing Adren to do the same, a kind of handshake with intent.

"You are forever at her side, young man. She is the thirteenth book. She absolutely is your destiny. Rhetoric will stop at nothing to control all the books, and again, that means hers most of all." Quinn tightened his grip, then released it all together, and smiled. "However, she is my daughters' daughter, head strong, stubborn and she does not listen. Have fun with that!"

They both chuckled and Quinn added, "She is also spirited and brave like both her parents, a dangerous mixture that could cause her to jump before thinking."

Adren nodded, "I understand, sir,"

Madrena was suddenly up at his side, quickly pecking her grandfather's cheek, then turning to Adren. "The page is ready."

He smiled, not just at her beauty and the way her eyes were sparkling once more, but at her bravery and lack of hesitation to aid those she loved.

"Then let's go!" said Adren taking her hand.

…And with that they flew up and into the book once more, as Quinn looked on in amazement. It was the first time he had witnessed the power of any of the books. So far, everything seemed to be going as he had envisioned so many years ago, but some things he had not foreseen…like the elk, and the love he had seen growing between his granddaughter and Adren.

He had barely returned home when they returned, the last two books remaining in hand. "That was quick!" he said.

Madrena looked into his eyes, "It was so quiet grandfather, so quiet," she paused, tears once again filling her green eyes. "The soldier faeries have been killed, only these two books were on the shelf as my parents said."

Quinn's lips pursed tightly together for just a moment before he replied. "Rhetoric has been busy. He must have the other ten, and the faeries attached to them."

The three stood in silence for a moment. Madrena had changed her clothes from the nightgown she had been wearing to tights and a mauve colored outfit, with boots that extended over her knees, banded with leather ties at the thigh. A shawl like her mothers hung down just to the top of them, her sword as well as two others on her back. She removed them now, handing them over to Adren as she stood with her back strong, eyes serious and said to her grandfather, "These were lying next to my father's desk. I believe they are Fire and Smoke's." Her eyes left the swords and she continued, saying to Adren, "We will need supplies. I will go and gather them."

She was just about through the doorway when her

grandfather added, "There is a pouch on my dresser, my dear, please bring it to me."

She turned, "A pouch?" one eyebrow arched like her mother showing her interest.

"Yes, just something I need you to deliver to Rhetoric."

Madrena headed through the doorway once more, a half smile now accompanying the arch of her brow and Quinn spoke again, "Where is *your* book my dear?"

Madrena paused turning back toward him, a full smile now came to her face and she pointed toward her own head. "Here grandfather, here."

She had barely cleared the doorway when she heard him say to Adren, "What do you know, the women in my family do listen!" Both men chuckled, and if they could have seen her face, they would have seen that she was still smiling.

"We put her book and the other two in the cave with the trunk," Adren said. "It is amazing, the way the book and she are linked. She says she can see the glow of the pages as they turn in her mind." The room fell silent as both men thought of what he had just said. The transparent Quinn watched as Adren did some last minute sharpening of all the swords. His eyes landed on the dragonfly dagger. "May I?" he asked pointing to it.

"Absolutely, sir," responded the dragonfly faerie as he met his eyes, adding, "But be careful, this dagger is said to be the one weapon that can kill a true magician."

The silver haired ends of Quinn's mustache curled upward showing the appreciation of his humor. "You have taken very good care of it," he said turning it over and over in his hands.

"It was a gift from my parents," replied Adren, looking up at him once more, one eye squinting and he continued. "You are the one who gave it them. You are the one who told them of my destiny, the one in the stories that they told me as a child."

Quinn pulled his eyes from the dagger for just a moment, catching his and said simply, "Yes."

Gently he placed the dagger back in Adren's hands then walked over pulling a chair from the corner of the room and sat down. "You and that dagger together play a large part in the defeat of Rhetoric." He held up his hand when Adren started to say something and continued, "I do not know how or when, just that it is and will be."

The young dragonfly faerie briefly lowered his eyes in thought, then looking straight back at Quinn he said, "I do not know how or when either, but I will be there."

The elderly magician stood, now rested, and placed a hand on Adren's shoulder who could barely feel it, answering, "I believe. I have always, and will always believe."

Madrena silently walked through the open doorway, supplies in one hand, pouch in the other, startling them both. "Sorry to interrupt this moment of male bonding, boys," she stated with a playful smirk on her face, "But we must be on our way."

"First things first my dear, please set down your supplies," her grandfather asked and she did so. "Open the pouch Madrena."

Slowly she loosened the drawstring that kept it closed, peering inside. It was a book, a very small one. The writing was even smaller; she was just able to read its cover. Once read, she quickly cinched it closed, looking up at her grandfather with questioning eyes.

"It will keep him busy until it is needed," was his only response. Madrena stared at him for a long moment, sure of one thing, there was something else; something he was not telling her. There were times she could not read his mind. As if his thoughts were behind some locked door she could not enter. She tied the pouch to her waist.

Adren stood, handing her sword to her with a slight nod of his head. She slid it into the sheath on her back, the pouch temporarily forgotten and they both turned to Quinn.

"We will return," Adren started, but Madrena finished, saying, "And tell you all the gory details of how Rhetoric was defeated!"

Her grandfather smiled at her. "Be safe and tell your mother and father I said hello." They hugged. "What no book to dive into?" he asked.

One eyebrow went up as she turned taking Adren's hand and looked back at him pointing to her head. "Flipping through the pages now and that won't take long," she laughed aloud. "There's not that many!" and they were gone!

Quinn smiled as they vanished, thinking, "Oh there are many, many pages my dear. You just haven't flipped them yet." He sat back down on the chair he had sat in before noticing his left foot as it faded away and reappeared, then a hand, followed by his entire right leg. Quinn looked over at the spot where Adren and Madrena had just stood. "Believe you two, for we are all counting on you," he said in almost a whisper as he slowly faded from view, leaving only his shawl lying on the floor in his beloved Quiviera.

CHAPTER X

Arrival of the Crown

THEY TRAVELED down the corridor of green meadows in silence for some time, following the path both were sure her parents had traveled as well. While Adren watched ahead Madrena was deep in thought marveling at the power of the thirteenth book, and its ability to appear in her arms when she called it. How by just her remembering this place, and the page in the book, that it had taken them there, realizing completely now what grandfather had meant when he said it was, "…in here."

The half smile appeared and she looked over at the handsome dragonfly faerie that somehow she knew was now and forever more to be part of her life. "Adren," she said placing her hand lightly on his arm.

He looked her way and in the same motion slid her hand into his. "Yes Madrena?"

She smiled glancing down at their clasped hands, then back up at him as they continued walking. "Grandfather told me the thirteenth book and I were linked; that each of us complimented the other's power; that from this time forward it would continue to record each adventure that lay before you and I, allowing me to access any memory in time of need."

He stopped now, stopping her, turning her fully toward him, taking her other hand in his.

"What are your memories of Rhetoric?"

"My memories of Rhetoric are only before the book, merely lessons and remarks through the years." She paused, gazing down the meadow with unseeing eyes. "The book, as grandfather said; is in here," she continued, pointing briefly at her head. "The first page is the cave when we met." She felt the heat of a blush come to her cheeks, smiled and continued again. "The last written page is Quiviera and grandfather."

Adren touched her cheek, following her chin line saying, "Those are not the only pages written, the last page is here. Right now it is being written. Since you and the book are linked as your grandfather says then it is making record of every thought you have. When you think back on the lessons and the remarks made in the past, the book makes note of them and adds them into that incredible reference library of memories; so even your first page is changing constantly and will for some time."

His thumb was on her chin now and they briefly swam in each others eyes.

"I am sure," added Adren, "That once we have defeated Rhetoric, there will be even more pages and then more and more as our lives go on."

"You said our," she broke in, feeling the heat of the blush once more.

There was no pause for thought, his answer came swiftly, "You are my destiny." ...and then he kissed her, soft and sweet, yet long and sensuous, and she kissed him back.

They separated looking deeply into each other eyes, both feeling the love that was growing. If, it were not for the familiar rasping screech of Cedrick above, they would have stood there mesmerized even longer.

"Ceddie?" questioned Madrena, squinting upward.

Adren looked up too shading his eyes as well from the late afternoon sun.

"I believe that is your friend," he replied.

"Yes, it is!" she answered excitedly waving her arm in the air as the great hawk began his descent down towards them. He landed on the ground at her feet, and she knelt stroking the great bird on his neck.

"Hello my friend, how did you find us?" Cedrick answered in a lower version of the rasping screech that had been heard from above. Adren watched, fascinated how Madrena seemed to understand everything the huge bird was saying, noticing the note strapped to its leg with a strand of leather.

He waited until they were finished. "You can understand him?" he asked.

"Yes," she answered, quickly holding up a finger, asking him to hold on.

Madrena asked the hawk a few more questions. At one point Cedrick must have asked who he was, for she said his name and that made him smile. He liked it when she said it. Madrena said good bye to him and the great bird nodded, first at her then towards Adren and he was up, flying off the way they had just come. Adren watched as he flew off, noticing this. He looked back the way they were going and then back over his shoulder at the great bird as he flew farther and farther away.

"Are we not headed in the right direction?" he asked.

Madrena took his hand, turning him back in the direction they had been heading.

"Let us fly for awhile. Cedrick says my parents and the others are but a half day ahead of us."

Adren pointed back over his shoulder, "Where is he headed then?"

Madrena's head turned looking back at her friend, a serious look in her eyes as the huge hawk soared higher and higher, answering, "Hopefully on a successful mission."

As both of their feet left the ground she told him what she and Cedrick had talked about…about Cinq, Saynk, and Sunck, and why the note was tied to his leg.

They flew for a short time side by side and then Adren carried her further yet while she rested her wings. He held her by the waist just below him, her back at him, her beautiful hair hitting his chest as they moved closer and closer to her parents and their troop of faeries. Were the elk still with them? They would find out soon enough.

* * *

Cedrick flew high above the pond where they had left their friends. He had been circling for some time now and had seen no sign of them as of yet. Down he went, landing on a rock just at the ponds' edge. He stared at the water, as if at any moment they would surface. What was it that he had heard Ciera tell Madrena when she was small and waiting for the cup of hot chocolate she loved so much, oh! A watched pot never boils, my dear. That was it.

Cedrick looked up to the vast sky above, craving the freedom it provided and wandered off in his mind thinking of Rhetoric and of older days when he thought as Rhetoric himself did now. Of days before his Queen, of days when there was no conscious, no remorse of deeds done, and no guilt felt at any time. His talons, weapons of destruction without hesitation, till the day he was saved by Ciera herself.

Blinking his eyes he briefly eyed the pond once more…no sign…not a single bubble nor any ripples, then looked upward. Effortlessly he rose into the blue above remembering more of the past, of the albatross and he wondered if his friend Karnan was still alive and well. His eyes shot back to the pond and he flew back down to the rock, first things first. He would wait for a sign from Cinq, Saynk, and Sunck as ordered by his queen. The water still showed no signs of change, not a single ripple moved across its glassy top. He closed his eyes settling down on the rock, napping while he waited and dreamed of Karnan, Ciera, and long ago.

He had been young and full of himself, free of allegiance to anyone…his only desire, to rule the skies. Only one species of bird had not yet submitted to him, the albatross. Their leader, Karnan had openly mocked him that it would never happen. Angered, Cedrick had challenged him and he had accepted.

The fight had lasted for hours. Both were bloody and scarred when Ciera had suddenly appeared between them, sword drawn, wings spread wide.

"As Queen of the Faeries I command you both to stand down!" She had taken them both by surprise, startling them.

Cedrick had been the first to recover saying, "I take orders from no one!" with a rasping shrill, his own wings spread wide. "Who are you to give me one?"

The beautiful faerie had replied swiftly and proudly, staring directly at him, showing not one sign of fear, "I am Ciera, the balance of Good and Evil."

With a quick motion she had bravely lifted her sword over her head and slid it gently into its sheath, then held her hands up. "I come not to fight unless I have too." Her eyes narrowed now, once more staring straight at Cedrick.

Immediately he had thought, "And you will lose," and in his mind he had heard her swift reply, "I will not."

Her left eyebrow had risen, a half smile had come to her face and he had known she could hear his thoughts.

Ciera continued aloud, "Give me just ten minutes of your time. Let me tell a short story of times to come. If you do not want to see as I do, well then, I will leave you both to continue this useless fight."

Karnan, who had been quiet till now, spoke, "Ciera, Queen of Faeries, I fight for the continued freedom of the Albatross nation. I do not see that as a useless fight."

His words were firm and true. Ciera looked his way, "You are right, Karnan."

The huge albatross spread his own wings now, his span greater than either hers or Cedrick by far, knitting his eyebrows in recognition of his name. "You have ten minutes," he responded.

She then had turned back to him, "And you Cedrick, will you give me ten?" He too heard his name. Who was this woman and how is it that she knows my name and Karnan's? A quick glance over to the great Albatross revealed he was pretty much thinking the same thing. He narrowed his eyes at her answer, "I will give you five."

So with Ciera between them, they both had listened to a story of the future and how one day they would need one another to help save life as it would be then. How their friendship, strength and belief in the right things would be crucial. Her five minutes up, she had then turned toward Cedrick, pulling her sword with her right hand, holding it down and off to the side. He remembered in his dream how her blue eyes had sparkled, how he could see the bravery she possessed.

"It is you Cedrick that must agree to settle this fight and realize that just as you love the freedom of the sky above, all who live under it are free as well. Karnan fights on the side of right, the side of good, protecting his kind and their future already. I do not need his answer. He will be there when needed." She had nodded toward Karnan and then turned back once again, toward him, sword still in hand. "You Cedrick however, fight for yourself, on the side of evil, and although I know these things about the future, I know that your fight now for submission of the Albatross and all others is wrong. I will protect the good and fight you now if necessary."

He remembered glancing over at Karnan. The gash over his eye was bleeding profusely, the rip in his left wing resembling the one in his own, also bleeding badly. A fight now against the faerie queen might be his last by her stance and obvious bravery. His eyes locked with hers and he knew he felt it. She had read his thoughts again.

"Your answer, Cedrick!" she commanded firmly.

"I will stop this fight for now. I will watch and see what the future brings." He had responded by moving his right wing in, then slowly outward again as he bowed in ascent. Ciera once again with a fluid motion had replaced her sword in its sheath, her eyes never leaving his. "As the Guardian of Good and Evil I must believe you for now, but guard you I will until your true colors show through as the great hawk you could become. Know that from this day forward I will see as you do and what you do. I will hear you from afar and our thoughts will be as one," ...and they had throughout the many years. Through countless adventures they had become close friends and Ciera had indeed seen his true colors. Even he and Karnan had become closer. All thanks to his Queen, his life had purpose and meaning. As his dream faded and his mind became clearer a question formed that had only one answer. Was it time to contact Karnan? The answer was yes.

Cedrick opened his eyes blinking away the sleep from his nap and heard the splashing as he did. It was her incredible lavender eyes that he had seen first, but it was Cinq's smile that had told him she was going to be okay. While one crack was still visible on her left cheek, it seemed to be healing even as all three emerged from the pond and said their hellos.

The great hawk screeched back, scratching the rock, bringing their attention to the note tied to his leg. Saynk was the first to react, quickly untying it and holding it up for Cinq and Sunck to see as well. Inside was a map to where Enol, their queen, and the others would be camping that night, as well as the location of three ponds along the way, and at the bottom in big letters was written:

HURRY! THE FIFTH MORNING APPROACHES!

They wasted no time flying off in the direction of the others and the first pond, but Cedrick had not followed them. He had flown toward the east, and Sunck questioned his sister and brother, as to why. Cinq answered, her voice cracking, not yet fully healed, "The map was intended for us, our queen must have something else in mind for him." Saynk had been quick to agree that she was right of course. Cedrick needed no map. Sunck, the oldest of the three, looked over to his sister as they flew on towards the first pond, noticing the crack still on her cheek. "You are not well as of yet. We will stop at each pond."

Her answer came swiftly as he had expected knowing how stubborn she could be. "Nonsense! I feel fine. The second pond will come soon enough for me."

Saynk sided immediately with his brother, having heard the cracking in her voice as well. "Consider yourself out voted sis, each pond it will be!"

Sunck started laughing now, and both Saynk and Cinq turned to him, waiting for the wisecrack they knew was coming. "Besides," he started, "There is one big faerie by the name of Sneakin I do not want to answer to if he thinks we have not taken excellent care of you!"

Redness swept quickly across Cinq's cheeks, a smile coming to her face, making both brothers laugh now. "Fine," she answered their laughter, "The first pond it is."

* * *

Cedrick glanced back at the three as their laughter carried on the wind with a quick thought of how happy he was and the others would be that they were better. His wings carried him higher, as he thought of his now friend, Karnan. This time of year he knew they would be nesting around the Lost Islands of Luree. A place made famous by a rebel of the same name, but that is another story for another time. He and the other albatross would be awaiting their young to grow and learn to fly, at which time they would return to the ocean winds. It was not too far now. He could just see the edge of the first island through the clouds.

* * *

A black striped fist slammed against the table causing the mist that sat on its top to move, almost jump as Anya finished her report from the captain of the ravens, who had just returned. No trunk and no thirteenth book in hand. There had been two books on the shelf but they had been unable to pick them up. They had not been able to move them at all in fact.

Rhetoric stared at the hallway that led to where ten books and the faeries bound to them were. It had been close. They had stood there surprised as he opened the door of the turret room, blinded by the light. He and Anya had been able to overpower them. Backing them up near the wall against the protest of the first two faeries, and the mist had taken over from there.

"There is one thing however they did bring back my dear Rhetoric," said Anya regaining his attention. She turned full circle bringing something up to her head, something that sparkled even in the dim light of the room, and faced him once more. The first thing he noticed was the triscale, a symbol of magic…the magic of the Old Ones.

His eyes narrowed as he noticed the emeralds and without warning he shot a strand of the mist at her head, pulling the crown back to him, yanking Anya's hair in the process. "Ow!" she yelled as strands of it accompanied the crown into his hands. He paid no mind to her, never looking up. He was too busy counting the emeralds, too busy wondering who the crown was meant for.

Rhetoric flashed his eyes at Anya, no sympathy was contained in them for her pain.

"Tell the ravens to rest now. They will be called on soon."

The evil twin of Ciera did not move, asking, "…And the crown?" She paused, careful in her choice of words, having seen the zombies of Anhur and IBNot controlled by the mist, and not wanting to become one. "May I hold it for you?"

He surprised her, tossing it to her. Rhetoric stared at her as she put it back on her head almost making her nervous.

"That crown almost looks good on you Anya, like it was made for you and your green…" His mouth snapped shut realizing, hearing his own words; and he turned back to the table once again, gazing into the puddle of mist that lay on it, muttering, "I must find IBNot," …and he did.

CHAPTER XI

The Fortress of Rhetoric

THE SHADES of darkness were approaching fast, the wind was getting worse, and the rain remained unrelenting. Their hair, wet as it was, slapped then stuck then slapped again at the sides of their faces, stinging their eyes repeatedly, but Ciera and Enol did not care. The dream Logren had shared with them shortly after departing camp this morning made everything else insignificant.

In his dream that night a young woman, a faerie; stood before him and in her arms were two books. The books had been old and leather bound; he had not been able to read the writing on them.

"She is alive!" Ciera had almost screamed.

"And she has the last two books," added Enol. His face had the biggest of grins.

Logren smiled at them both. "The young woman, your daughter?" he asked.

Ciera questioned his question, "Purple red hair?"

"Why yes," Logren had replied quickly, once again causing a smile to form on her face. The kind that was hard to lose.

"My daughter is learning quickly, my new friend," Ciera said, placing her hand gently on his shoulder. "Yesterday, when we talked of the books and their disappearance from Whisper Hollow, you felt something, and thought you sensed something."

The muscles in the eyes of the great elk tensed up, "Yes, that something or someone was there, though nothing could be seen."

Ciera stepped back from Logren explaining, "It was Madrena. She and I, well...we can sort of take ourselves, project ourselves to a place we need to be. We cannot do anything or talk to anyone. We can only watch and learn, as my daughter must have where it concerns the last two books."

She hesitated briefly looking towards Enol, he was smiling and he continued for her. "If Madrena was able to obtain and secure the last two books, then she is free and not being held by Rhetoric. Sneakin and Peakin as well as Cinq, Saynk, and Sunck are not in danger."

He paused, his full smile now becoming that familiar half grin and Ciera raised her eyebrow when she saw it. "Something else to add my love?" she asked.

Enol's smile broadened again. "I was just thinking; when Madrena heard what she heard about the books, well, that was just a little more than one day ago. If Logren dreamed of her holding the books last night, our daughter has been busy. Either she has help or she is able to project and do more than just watch and hear, or both, for she has those books."

Ciera pushed her eyebrow even higher as she inhaled almost whispering, "The thirteenth book..."

Enol's smile remained, his lips pressed together, and both of his eyebrows had risen. There was no reason to respond, she knew he agreed.

On that good note, they had begun the day's travel; a little less worried, a little more light hearted at the news of Madrena being safe. A little more assured and hopeful that they would be triumphant in the end. Throughout the day, they followed the Tube River at their left as it flowed toward their destination. The raging torrent of water weaved itself down the path it had cut through the canyon.

Ciera, Enol, their small band of faeries, and the elk looked forward. They had finally arrived and before them lay their next challenge. A sea of black mist that started just ahead covered the ground in its entirety…or was it water? To the left, the Tube and now to the right, another river of equally rough water could be seen flowing into it, with the two of them seeming to become one.

Enol looked over to Ciera with one eyebrow raised and a half grin. "I can only imagine what is really out there."

His wife looked over at him cocking her own eyebrow, "Keep imagining, my dear; and multiply it by ten times worse with the looks of it."

Enol sniffed the air. "I smell salt.

Ciera pointed towards the water on the right, "The Zacarra. It is pushed by the ocean and brings the salt with it…undrinkable." Then she pointed towards the body of water that had been on their left most of the day. "The Tube however, flows from the mountains bringing drinkable water."

Enol broke in, "So one is good and one is bad?"

Her eyebrow rose again as she looked over at him. Just the smallest part of the corner of her mouth curling into that familiar smile, showing she heard the pun, "Funny! These are not the kind of good and bad that I can control."

The hillside they stood on was littered with enormous boulders. Ciera climbed on top of one of the largest, waving their small troop over as she pointed down at their last obstacle.

"As before, this is not what it seems. Once as with the Forest of Fire, there were beautiful trees here, grass and flowers, birds and other wildlife, but the evil of Rhetoric possesses it now, and uses it for protection. Look! The fortress evil calls home!"

They all stared at the dark outline of the castle. Its tall turrets were now barely visible, silhouetted against the coming sunset, nearly hidden by the black clouds that encircled them. The body of the fortress itself was nearly hidden by the black mist that surrounded it. All that could be truly distinguished were the remnants of once great trees that littered its base, all black and gray in color, just visible above the even blacker sea of mist.

Ciera watched as they stared at the home of Rhetoric. She saw anger in the eyes of them all as well as longing in the eyes of Logren's wife, Maleah, and added, "We are close, my friends; closer than ever to rescuing our loved ones, and defeating the likes of IBNot and Rhetoric but we must rest awhile, prepare and await the arrival of the Wind Riders."

The antlers of the great elk cut and thrashed the air as they snorted thinking of their young, and Logren's voice thundered, "Why wait? Let us move forward to the castle now!"

Ciera looked over at him, her eyes softening, but still showing the strength she possessed. "My sentiments exactly, my dear Logren; but first we must know the way. Below this mist the two rivers meet, separated only by a natural wall of stone, their waters never mixing. It is yours, Logren, and Maleah's, Tarin's and the other Amberwood faeries, as well as my husbands' way in." She turned to face the fortress and the mist, looking back over her shoulder at them all, adding, "The trick will be finding that wall."

"That could prove difficult to do," Enol said to her.

She glanced over her shoulder again at him, past Nip, who was now sitting there clinging to her shawl in the strong wind, then back again to her small friend. "Maybe not, I have an idea," and she whispered in the furry ear of Nip who promptly disappeared in the folds of her shawl.

The great elk ceased his snorting, but continued breathing heavily; as he watched Ciera place her hand beneath her shawl pulling forth both Nip and Tuck and kneel on the giant boulder placing them upon it. They scurried off, their fur blowing in the wind, running directly toward the black mist and disappearing under it.

"The wall you must travel on to reach Rhetorics fortress is somewhere under the mist. It will be a narrow path and the waters from both rivers will slam against its sides, splashing upon it, threatening to sweep all who attempt to cross it to their death. My little friends will find it and while they do we will rest and regain our strength for what is to come."

The great elk snorted once more, he knew she was right, that they must wait, but he did not want to. Ciera continued, looking not only at him but addressing the other elk as well. "I know you are as anxious to save your children as we are to save our friends. Nip and Tuck will mark the way to the wall. Darkness falls and we are not many…one wrong step," she paused, "We cannot risk losing anyone."

Enol had taken her hand, and he squeezed it as she paused again, looking into the eyes of her comrades. "Let us make camp and prepare."

She caught Peakin's attention, winking at her. "Peakin has promised a batch of her famous mushroom soup, we will meet fireside in one…" but Ciera stopped mid sentence. She stared at Sneakin who was staring intently behind her. Something from the mist had caught his eye. She turned and saw. Something or someone was moving out of it, up into the sky.

Enol stared briefly at his wife noticing her eyes, and followed her line of site, seeing the blackness that rose from the mist as well. "What the heck is that?"

All eyes watched as the mass of black rose completely out of the mist, now silhouetted by the evening sky. Ciera looked side to side at the two rivers and at the few trees that stood between them that could be considered cover. She glanced over at Enol as he pointed back toward the mass…it was separating.

The silence was broken by Maleah. "Ravens, they are ravens!" she yelled.

The Queen of the Faeries and her knight magician pulled their swords simultaneously. "Prepare yourselves my friends, I promise these guys are not just coming for tea!" roared Enol. Logren and the other elk bravely moved in front of the group of faeries forming a barrier between them and the ravens. "Get to the trees my friends, we will hold them off!" he yelled back. The great elk barely had time to turn back when the first wave of ravens hit. They came fast and hard. One elk was knocked to the ground by a large group of them, as everyone ran towards the trees. A second wave was upon the elk now, and then instantly a third. Even Logren had trouble holding his ground

It was the fourth wave that reached Ciera, Enol, and Sneakin and Peakin and they were the largest of all. Ten times the size of the ones that were now fighting the others, and keeping the Amberwood faeries in the boughs of the trees above them. Each of these ravens were easily as tall as each of them, they fought them one on one.

Sneakin had spread his wings fighting in mid air with his own sword, and Piggett's, barely fending off the long sharp talons of a huge bird as it used his beak as well, stabbing at him at every chance.

Enol stood with his back against a tree, the beak of the raven he was fighting barely missing his face gouging the tree behind him. He was in trouble and Ciera saw it.

"I am done playing with you now," she said to the raven in front of her.

She swung her sword high at its beak and as the raven leaned backwards to avoid it, he in turn lashed out with the talons of his right claw. Ciera's sword swung full circle, cutting off the entire claw before the bird could withdraw it and immediately he flew back toward the mist.

She turned running toward her husband, who was now pinned through the thigh to the tree by the talons of the bird he fought, his sword held firmly in its beak.

"Get away from him!" she yelled, her sword high.

Enol looked up pain rippling through his body from the talon that speared his thigh. "No!" he yelled loudly as he looked past her, behind her.

Ciera saw the look of warning on his face, but not the two ravens behind her, till their talons secured each arm, lifting her into the air, while the one on the right snatched her sword from her, tossing it to the ground. No one could help her. They were all fighting for their own lives. The ravens that held her turned flying toward the mist, disappearing within it.

Instantly the rest of the ravens flew up, hovering just overhead, all except one, the one that held Enol. Sneakin and the others ran toward them both, but stopped short with swords drawn, as the huge raven turned its head and spoke.

"With one twist of this sword I could cut off his head. Do not come any closer." He then turned his attention to Enol, slowly withdrawing the talon from his thigh so as to cause more pain, then quickly took the sword from his beak, and held it at Enol's throat. He talked loudly for the others to hear. "I have explicit instructions not to hurt you, seems my master wants you all to himself." The raven backed away slowly.

"Where have you taken my wife?" Enol asked.

The huge bird's eyes squinted, and he smiled, "She has family in these parts, someone wants to see her." He said it snidely as he rose in the air, tossing the sword at Enol's feet, causing it to stab the ground. "Do not follow, I love disobeying my master," and with that he flew away leading the other ravens, disappearing into the mist, while Enol and the others could only stand and watch.

CHAPTER XII

Allies on the Inside

TEN BOOKS were now stacked on the floor, just out of reach of Fire and Smoke. The faeries attached to the other nine had arrived with their books. They had been surprised by Rhetoric and Anya *and the mist*, and now twenty three in all, including Night and Day stood shackled to the wall.

The light faded from the open turret above, as sunset came and they became immersed in darkness. The tiniest faerie of them all turned up the volume, lighting up the round room. Skinnie was the first to speak, he was careful of his words. Black mist crept from under the door. Was Rhetoric listening just on the other side?

"Any luck, Fire?"

"No;" he came back simply.

He had tried and tried for some time before the rest of them had arrived but the heat he was able to generate from his body did not affect the black metal that shackled their wrists to the wall; in fact, not even a single blemish had appeared on it.

"There must be something about it, no amount of heat I generate seems to start to bend it, much less melt it," added Fire.

"Maybe it is not metal." Night said, slow and deliberately, and all eyes turned towards him. He lowered his head towards his own shackles, and continued, "If you could see what we think is metal from over here, in the brightness of my sisters light, you would see that it moves."

Day's eyes went from her brothers shackles to her own, "He is right! It does move!"

There was a quick glance shared between Fire and Smoke, both were thinking the same thought, "We did feel it move before."

Night continued, turning full attention to Skinnie, "I saw you look towards the door before you questioned Fire about his efforts. There is no one out there. I have been watching the door for a while, as well as the black mist that creeps under it. No one is there." Fire looked at the black mist then back at the small dark faerie.

"What are you getting at, Night?"

"Watch the mist as it slips through. Where does it go?" The dark faerie smiled a small smile. Fire and the others all looked over, following the path of the black mist as it went up the door halfway, then split in two, continuing along the stone walls, traveling towards each and every one of their shackles.

"They are connected!" Fire almost shouted.

"Yes," answered Night simply. "The mist and our shackles are one, fed and reinforced by that continuous flow of mist."

Piggett squealed, "No way. It cannot be that easy!" Her brother Hyde and the others looked around the room, all eyes questioning what she meant.

"It will not be easy, my dear Piggett," Night replied simply and quickly. Her eyes scanned the books and the distance between them and the door.

"You are right my friend," she answered.

"What will not be easy?" burst out Hyde finally.

Fire spoke up, "Breaking the connection." ...and it would not be easy, as there was nothing in the room except for them, and their books of course; and they were stacked just out of reach. Soon silence prevailed, as all twenty three stared at the mist, desperately trying to figure out a way to break the connection, and free them all. They did not see the mass of blackness that flew in and out of the mist over the turrets above, or the two huge hawks that held their beloved queen. Day's light faded, she must rejuvenate. Darkness prevailed once more.

* * *

The talons of the huge ravens were like vices around her wrists, holding her tightly. Ciera could not and did not resist. The black mist obscured everything, what was below and ahead. "How did these birds know the way?" she wondered. Then, as suddenly as they had entered the mist, they were free of it, traveling over the turret tops of Rhetorics fortress. There were five of them...was that a light deep down in the second turret? She had barely caught a glimpse of it.

Just as Cedrick did back home, they circled first before bringing her down at the front gates, letting go of her as they passed some five feet from the ground. She landed hard, rolling, but automatically came to a standing position, pulling the dragonfly dagger, her only weapon, as she did.

The black mist that hugged the ground stuck to her like dirt, and she brushed at it as she looked around. Everything had the stuff on it, even the air seemed full of it, and it even dimmed her vision somewhat.

"Don't worry, it only sticks to bad people," came a voice from behind blackened trees about ten feet away. Ciera smiled her half smile, her eyebrow rising, she knew that voice.

"You must be covered in it then, my sister!" However, the smile left her face as the voice stepped into view.

In many ways she still loved the sister of her memories and hated seeing what stood before her now, but Anya was a big girl and she had made her choice many years before. Thick black lines spiraled down her body, disappearing only briefly under the leather collar around her neck and scant garb she wore, even her hair was streaked with the blackness.

"Now, now…" her sister said snidely. "Where did that smile go Ciera? You are not feeling sorry for me are you?" Anya stood straight and strong, tall and thin, a sword in her left hand and what looked to be a whip in the other. The black lines that ran down her face seem to start at her hairline extending downward toward her eyes, curling around them, disappearing once more into the hairline, only to reemerge on her lower cheek, and cascade downward toward her neck and chest. Sisters and twins, they were identical in every way except for the stripes and the damage caused by the mist and of course, Madrena's crown on her head.

"Sorry for you? Oh no," Ciera responded clearing her throat. She must not let her see that she recognized the crown. "Your choice of life is your own, but if we were talking ashamed of? Absolutely!" She held the dagger at her side ready for something, anything to happen in response to the insult. She did not want to waste its virgin blade on Anya, but it was the only weapon she had. "You hold your dagger as though you are poised for action, my sister;" Anya said, her voice now sultry. "I just found out there was family in the area and thought we should visit."

Ciera smiled at her, showing she was unafraid. "And what, sister; would we have to visit about?" The whip hit her hand quickly, its gnarled end wrapping around the dagger. Ciera pulled back hard, trying to cut through it with the blade. Anya charged, her sword high, winding the whip around her own arm as she descended upon Ciera, ready to serve a final blow as she yelled, "Maybe we could discuss who should really be Queen of the Faeries!"

However her sword never met its mark. Ciera was suddenly thrown back towards the gray black rock foundation that supported the fortress. Anya's whip, still wrapped around the dagger, wrenched it from her hand. She landed hard, dead center against the second rock up, but did not fall from it…it was as though she was glued to it. Blackness covered her torso, arms and legs. Struggling was useless. Some twenty feet away she could see Anya talking to a dark figure, nearly twice her size. Rhetoric! She could not hear what they were saying, but could tell they were both angry. Her sister threw a disgusted glance at her. Even through the mist she could see the fire in those eyes as Anya walked toward her, the dragonfly dagger in her hand now and the dark figure of Rhetoric, who followed. She must retrieve the dagger! Both stood before her now, illuminated by a grayish glow that seemed to emanate from the rocks of the foundation. Their stripes were even more vivid now… and they moved.

Ciera started, "My dear Rhetoric, it has been years! You've changed."

His response was swift, and he almost snarled when he spoke. "For the better I think, Ciera." He paused, turning to the right then to the left tracing his outline with extended forefingers, as if modeling then continued. "You and yours are almost a memory now. With the old man gone the only thing standing in my way for complete control of all the books is your husband and word from my head raven, is that he has been injured."

He paused again, waiting for the hurt and despair to fill her eyes that only evil thrives on, but Ciera showed him none. She set her jaw in disgust then smiled, looking over at Anya, "Hey sis! You two should have kids; you could name them Strip and Stripe!" ...and alone she laughed aloud. Wings flared and immediately her sister was upon her, and the tip of her own dragonfly dagger's blade was felt at her chin.

Anya smiled pulling Ciera's hair with her free hand, forcing her head to hit the rock.

"You're so funny." Her expression changed to the frozen grimace she had before and she continued. "He says I cannot kill you yet, that I must wait. That he needs you for both our dreams to come true."

Ciera set her jaw once more, staring directly into her sister's eyes. "Your dreams will never come true my sister. You will never be queen. That crown was never meant for the likes of you."

Anya's grip on the dagger tightened, her lips disappearing into the lines that traced her mouth. "And why not?"

Ciera's eyes never wavered from hers, "Because you are a follower, not the leader you were brought up to be."

With that, she tossed a glare towards Rhetoric, then turned fully to face her sister once more. "Where's your leash that fits that collar, sis!"

Anya was furious! She raised the dagger into the air, a crazed look on her face, shaking; yet frozen, as if torn on what she should do and what she wanted to do, furious that the decision was not hers to make and the knowledge that the leash remark was partially true.

Rhetoric yelled her name and in the same instant a stream of black mist hit the dagger, ripping it from her hand, bringing it straight into his own.

Ciera spit in Anya's face and she sprang backwards, her useless wings snapping in anger, trying to catch the air around them to hold her up. She wiped her face, glaring back at her sister then dropped to the ground landing beside Rhetoric, who continued looking up at Ciera, pointing at her. "You! Close that mouth…NOW! Your time is short, but I can make it shorter with another shot of mist that will cover your face, and smother you slowly."

The Queen of the Faeries answered with only a grimace showing disgust and Rhetoric shot forth another stream of the mist. Instinctively, Ciera slammed her eyes shut expecting the worst. She reopened them after feeling the blast hit not her face, but her mid torso, becoming one with the blackness that already held her, with Rhetoric in control. Slowly, she was moved down the huge stone until she was in the middle of the lower one, at eye level with him.

Rhetoric stepped forward and grabbed her right wrist with his left hand, pulling her from the stone as she watched some of the blackness retreat back into him and the rest fall away from her body, fading away into the cracks of the rock foundation at his touch. He pulled her inches from his face; his breath was foul, glancing over at the crown on Anya's head, saying, "My head raven retrieved this from your home," he paused looking at her intently, waiting for a sign, noticing her blue eyes. "If it is not meant for Anya who is it meant for?"

Ciera held his stare for a moment then responded sarcastically, "Oh! That old thing! Where did you find it? I have been looking everywhere for it!" The eyes of Rhetoric turned to slits. She never saw the fist that hit her.

* * *

Madrena saw her parent's camp as they flew over the last rolling hill, and Adren could feel her excitement to see them, as he held her by the waist. The rain had let up. Thank goodness. They were soaked through, and with the coolness of the night the campfires were a welcome sight.

He set her down not far from the camp, deciding to walk in so as not to startle anyone, but they had. Before Adren knew it Logren had him down on the ground, as he had Ciera.

"Friend or Foe?" he had thundered and Madrena answered from behind them both, "Friend!"

Without pulling his mighty hoof from just above Adren's head, he turned immediately towards her. "You!"

"Yes," she answered without talking.

The great elk's mouth curled in the corners and he turned to the faerie under his hoof and backed away, careful not to step on his wings, bowing slightly toward him, "I am Logren, forgive me, but I am sure you understand."

"Absolutely, I would have acted the same," he replied, picking himself up then bowing slightly back at him. "My name is Adren and this is Madrena."

Logren turned toward her, "It is my pleasure woman from my dream," once again the slight bow. Madrena smiled at him and he continued, "Your father is just over there, I am sure he is anxious to see you."

"And my mother?" returned Madrena. There was an unpleasant silence, and Adren seeing concern in the great elk's eyes turned toward her, taking one of her hands into both of his. "Go see your father. I will follow shortly, after I speak with Logren some more." Madrena nodded in agreement, her eyes turning serious. She turned slowly towards her father's tent, a million what ifs flying through her head. Both watched as she ran toward the tent and was safe inside.

Adren looked up at the great elk. As tall as he was himself, the top of Logren's head still loomed some three feet above him, and that did not include his huge rack which added another four feet. "My new friend, do you know what lies beyond?" He nodded his head toward the blackness that could be seen ahead, even in the dark of night.

"Rhetoric and his evil…and how is it that you are part of this fight." Logren replied, watching as the young dragonfly faeries' eyes darted toward the tent and he answered his own question. "Yes, she is beautiful, for a faerie of course."

Both smiled now, and they exchanged the short version of their stories. Just as they finished Madrena called over to them in thought.

Adren looked quickly over at Logren with a questioning look. "Did you hear something?"

The great elk smiled down at him, "Yes, but not in my ears, in my head!"

"Yes, I know, in mine as well!" His head turned toward Madrena's fathers' tent. This was something he had not known about her.

A smile came to his face as Logren replied, "Get used to it, friend. They do that a lot around here."

Together they walked over to the campfire, now occupied by Enol and the rest of the troop including Maleah, Logren's wife. Madrena stood at the side, somewhat out from the group, her sword still on her back. She introduced Adren to the group. The tone in her voice however was distant, as if she was thinking about something entirely different. Sneakin stood shaking his hand; welcoming nods came from the others as well, but all the while Madrena was silent. Adren looked away from the others, concern in his eyes now and started walking towards her.

"Stop Adren," she said it firmly, holding up her hand, turning her attention then to her father. "Please tell him everything you have told me."

Her eyes returned to Adren and she said, "Know that I love you and I will be back," And with that she was gone.

Her father shouted, "Madrena!" but she did not return. He

turned to the half dragonfly, half faerie and asked, "Where has she gone?"

"What did you tell her?" responded Adren. Enol looked deeply into the young mans' eyes, thinking of his daughter's parting remarks, particularly the 'I love you' part.

"Her mother was taken." His voice trailed off as tears formed in his eyes. "We have a lot to talk about young man."

"Yes I believe we do," replied Adren.

Peakin, who was handing out the mushroom soup she had prepared, did so with tears remembering the last request of her queen. She now handed a bowl to Adren and said. "Please sit, warm yourself, and eat. We will tell our story and you will tell yours."

Slowly he took the soup from her hand and sat, all the while staring at the spot Madrena had stood. "Your daughter," he looked at Enol, at the same time nodding towards the others, "And your princess, will return."

For a moment, all was silent as they ate; then Enol straightened his back and asked the first question, "How did you meet my daughter?" Adren smiled, looking out at the black mist, then back at him, "I feel I have known her forever..."

* * *

Madrena stood in the cave where her now beloved Adren had first taken her. She had to think. Water still trickled from the wall. The trunk still sat close by, with the thirteenth book on its lid. It was something that Adren had said...what was it? They had been in the meadow half a day back, and had been discussing the last page of the book. Yes! The book recorded my memories and lessons on its pages. Mom is a memory, but the place where she is, is not; but she could make it a memory, just as she had the first time she had seen the great elk, Logren, with her parents. Just as she had brought her and Adren back there, not as simple viewers, but in the flesh.

Madrena closed her eyes concentrating deeply. Immediately she felt the coolness of stone beneath her feet, and she opened her eyes, squinting as they adjusted to the darkened circular room. Mere traces of the moonbeams far above cut through the darkness, giving only minimal light to the floor below.

Tears formed as her eyes focused and she spotted her mother almost hanging from the wall, held by what looked like shackles around her arms and legs. She was unconscious.

"Mother!" Madrena whispered in her mind, "Wake up! I will return!"

She took a long look around seeing that it was a turret room that served as her mothers cell and vanished barely catching a glimpse of Ciera as she stirred and straightened, awakening and mumbling, "Madrena?"

Back she came in the flesh just as her and Adren had appeared in the meadow, stopping in the cave only long enough to check her sword and concentrate on the new page she had just created in her book. Madrena held her mothers' face gently in both hands, brushing back the stray hairs that had loosened from her braids.

"Mother, it is I, Madrena."

Ciera held her head up under her own power now, focusing her eyes, smiling, "But how my daughter?"

Madrena answered quickly. "Now is not the time. We must get you out of here first."

She looked towards what she had thought was shackles and saw the band of mist for what it was. Her eyes followed the trail that it wove to the door, then disappearing under it.

Ciera, now fully awake, watched as her daughter walked towards the door. She did not notice that the mist moved up and away from Madrena as she approached it.

"It is the mist of Rhetoric himself, he controls it. Do not

touch it."

Madrena turned, smiling at her mother, for she had notice it move up and away. "I do not think that will be an option, Mom. I do not think it likes me."

Her mother's eyebrow rose. It was true. As Madrena moved yet closer to the door, the mist moved higher up the stone wall, as if avoiding her. Ciera watched her daughter follow the mist back towards her wrists. "What are you thinking Madrena?" She saw the sparkle in her daughters' green eyes as she stood before her and she had to smile.

"I am thinking Mom that this mist is moving." Pausing, Madrena quickly put her hands down on either side of her mother's wrists, aiming directly at the flow of mist, but never touching it. It jumped away before she could, joining the strand that held Ciera's legs and Madrena continued, "And that by breaking the connection you will be free!"

Her mother grabbed her wrists, as remnants of the mist that had held them fell away disappearing into the cracks of the stone, and as she rubbed them Madrena hit the wall again. This time on either side of her ankles, causing the mist to crack like a whip against the wall and flee under the door, and free she was! Ciera spread her wings, stretching them, relieving the cramping from being smashed against the wall, noticing how they touched each side of the turret walls. "Well I guess we won't be flying out of here."

She walked over to one of the vines that fell from the turret opening above, pulling hard. "I think this is our way out," she said as her eyes followed it up the turret wall. Ledges about every ten feet could be seen all the way up.

Madrena just smiled over at her, "Mom, we are leaving here just the way I came in." Ciera's eyes went from her daughters to the turret wall and the vines. "And how was that?" she asked, but Madrena did not answer. She was no longer looking at her mother. She was looking at the door and the shadow that loomed under it, shooting itself out into the turret room and Ciera saw it too. Madrena started to move toward her mother, to grab her hand and be gone, but she stopped seeing the hook handle of the door turn.

She whispered instead loudly, a little too loudly, "Climb up mom, up the vines!"

The door swung open with Rhetoric saying snidely, "I heard the word mom," his eyes landing upon her. "Madrena? Is that really you? My, my…how you have grown up!"

His eyes seem to squint so much that they were mere slits on his face, his smile revealing mist damaged teeth. "I have had no reports from IBNot, or my ravens of you. I have wondered where you were."

Slowly he moved through the doorway, the room lighting up from the light outside momentarily then darkened again as his enormous size blocked it once more; keeping Madrena in his shadow.

Ciera had made it to the first level, ten feet above and yelled down, "Watch out for the mist! He shoots it from his hand, my daughter!"

Rhetoric shot her a quick glance, but returned his gaze back to Madrena remembering the mist and how it had recoiled so hard earlier, while he sat at his desk. That and how it had almost knocked him from the chair in which he had been sitting. His eyes once more turned to slits as he searched the dimness of the shadow for her eyes…for green, and found it.

"I think we may have a lot to talk about my dear. What do you know about a certain thirteenth book?"

Rhetoric took a step toward her then another, letting even more light fill the room; allowing Ciera to see the two thick strands of mist that trailed from his body and out the door. Madrena saw them too. Them, and the tapestry on the wall above her all rolled up, allowing its rope to hang down within grabbing distance.

She ignored his question about the thirteenth book, saying instead, "There is not and never will be a 'we' with us Rhetoric, and you will never have the thirteenth book."

Her mother added, "Ditto!"

He snarled first at Madrena then turned, glaring up at Ciera and Madrena bolted. The Queen of the Faeries watched breathlessly as her savior, her daughter; ran toward the opposite wall and jumped, grabbing the rope from the tapestry above, pulling herself upward. Loose rock fell the short distance to the floor as she tried to gain footing between the stones that made up the wall. She was almost there. Red yellow eyes flashed towards her then back towards Ciera briefly when she yelled, "You will die this night, Rhetoric; if you harm one hair on her head!"

He looked up at her snarling, "I am not afraid of you."

Ciera clung tightly to one of the vines that hung from the turret above as it shifted and moved with her weight, thinking of what to say to distract him so Madrena could make it up to the ledge.

"Maybe you are not, Rhetoric," she threw down, taunting him. "You were not afraid of my father either, but you and my sister lost then and you will lose now, in this once again quest for control of the books!" He looked up snorting, angered, stirring the mist that rose from the stones with the bottom of his cape as he turned from side to side.

Madrena, now balanced on the stone ledge just to the right of the doorway, remembered her recent lessons in Quiviera and angered him even more by saying, "Those stripes aren't tattoos are they Rhetoric? How many have appeared since you last saw grandfather? They are the kind of gift that keeps on giving, huh?"

The blackened figure of a man whirled around, looking up at her snorting again, almost growling, as Ciera climbed further up her vine behind him smiling, yet wondering how her daughter knew what she knew, and getting her answer immediately as it popped into her head.

"Grandfather, Mom!" causing Ciera to shoot a short stare at Madrena as she made her way up the turret wall to the next ledge and her daughter continued with Rhetoric.

"Mmm you've been busy! One bad deed equals one stripe! Yes, I'd say you have been a naughty, naughty boy."

Rhetoric snorted louder now, thoroughly angered, "How can you know this? You could not!" He threw his left hand toward her and blackness spewed forth splattering against the wall, just missing her. Rhetoric was so angry he did not notice that his aim had indeed been true. That the mist itself had changed its own course away from his target, but Madrena did, and so did her mother.

She pushed him more. "Grandfather told me."

She said it short and matter of fact. Rhetoric, who had been split between mother and daughter, now focused fully on Madrena, eyes once more mere slits, saying, "Impossible! That foolish magician died years ago when his beloved Quiviera faded! You must take me for a fool!" He snarled again, glancing down at the strands of mist trailing behind him, as if counting them, and Ciera noticed. Their eyes met and he turned running at the wall, hitting it just under the ledge on which Madrena stood. The wall shook violently, pieces of the ledge cracked, some crumbled.

She clung to the tapestry at her back yelling down at him, riling him even more.

"Not impossible! He told me just two days ago!"

The mist at Rhetoric's feet now seemed to rise as if steamy.

"Liar!" he screamed, ramming the wall again.

The stone beneath her left foot fell to the floor and Madrena watched as it shattered into small pebbles and powder, but once again she regained her footing by hanging onto the tapestry. She glanced over at her mother who had made her way up the vine even more, now standing in the shadows across the room on the ledge just above the one she herself stood on. Madrena yelled down again, keeping his attention as Ciera worked her way around the turret.

"And he gave me a present for you!"

He stared up at her with those red yellow eyes of his, and she continued, "Your own book!" With one hand holding tightly to the tapestry, she pulled the tiny book from the pouch on her waist, tossing it down at Rhetoric's feet. Ciera stopped, watching as the book fell and grew in size, reading the cover as it slammed on the floor below.

'The Book of Rhetoric'

The sound of ripping tapestry jerked her attention back to her daughter and she made her way quickly along the ledge till she was just above her, grabbing the last section of material, as it ripped free. Mother and daughter stared briefly at each other, eyes at their widest; both hearts pounding then back down at Rhetoric, who stared down with an angered but intrigued look at the book on the floor.

Neither could take their eyes off him as he bent over to examine it more closely. He reached toward it, an all but black thumb touched the lower corner of it as he knelt, playing with the thought…calculating the risk of opening its cover.

Suddenly he sprang to his feet flipping the book and pushing it to the opposite wall screaming as he did. "You cannot fool me. This is a trick!"

He flung his arm pointing up at Madrena causing his cape to snap sideways and he sent another stream of the black mist straight at her. She held up her hands to shield herself and her mother watched in amazement as the mist stopped in midair, flying instead straight back, straight back into Rhetoric's face and eyes, surprising him so completely that he stumbled backwards.

Ciera saw their chance and slid down the wall to a squat, careful to keep the tapestry taut with one hand to maintain her daughters balance, while reaching out to her with the other.

"Madrena!"

Their hands interlocked and Ciera pulled her up to the ledge alongside her, motioning to the vines and the open turret above. Madrena nodded in agreement but held up her finger asking for a moment more. She let go of the tapestry and it fluttered to the floor, catching Rhetoric's eye as he wiped the mist from them. He turned his gaze upward, his mouth open ready to speak, but Madrena did not give him the chance.

"No trick, Rhetoric. It is your book, meant for you alone."

A low rumbling growl like thunder seemed to come from somewhere within him as he turned to look at the book once more and Madrena continued, "Turn it over, check out the title again…open it."

The blackened, striped man was consumed with curiosity. He could not help it. He flipped the book with a wave of his hand, rereading the title he had already read, calculating the risk of opening it once more as mother and daughter moved quickly along the ledge to the vines and climbed their way to the turret above.

He noticed their ascent to late, splattering the walls with more of the black mist, breaking off the vines below them as they climbed, sending them crashing below around him.

They stood on the turret ledge both of their wings spread wide, filling with air, watching as Rhetoric shook his fist at them, snorting and grunting. He glared up at them as he walked toward the book that lay on the floor and roared up at them, "I will have the thirteenth book! I do not need the other two you have hidden! Yes, I know you somehow saved them!"

Madrena looked over towards her mother the corners of her mouth curling playfully, her eyes sparkling with playful mischief and she turned, yelling back down at him, "How do you know Rhetoric, maybe your book is the thirteenth book."

Rhetoric immediately glanced at the book, briefly contemplating this newest remark then back at the two of them, his fists clenched so tightly his palms bled as he roared a final long and loud roar up after them...but they were gone into the blackness he himself had created.

They flew straight up through it, mother and daughter, to the dim light they had seen from the ledge on which they had stood just moments before, to the fresh air. The final roar of Rhetoric could still be heard as they broke through the last of the mist into the starlit night sky.

Madrena turned to her mother laughing and pointing at her face, "I think you need a bath!"

Ciera pointed back at her saying, "Just imagine that right now you are looking in a mirror. Another words, so do you my dear!"

They hugged still laughing, their wings gently moving keeping them just above the black mist. Ciera took her daughters hands saying, "That book..." but Madrena broke in, "Not the thirteenth book but yes, a present from grandfather. It will keep him busy for a while." She smiled seeing questions in her mother's half smile and raised eyebrow and she added, "Boy mom, we have a lot to talk about!"

Ciera smiled fully now, "Yes dear, I should say we do!"

Slowly, enjoying each others' company they flew back toward the camp as Madrena told her mother everything that

had happened in the last four days, and Ciera told her everything, including about the crown with the triscale and the
thirteen emeralds.

* * *

Together they sat eating the mushroom soup Peakin delivered
to them both as soon as they had returned, and it was good,
warm and filling. The Queen of the Faeries cleared her throat
softly and dabbed a leaf to her lips, although no words came
through them. Her eyes came to rest on Adren whom she had
met promptly upon landing back at the campsite. She had
noticed the way Madrena's hand had slipped easily into to his,
and how he had accepted it just the same.

Ciera watched as he gently placed a blanket around her
daughter's shoulders and she asked him, "Adren, do you know
the name IBNot?" And the dragonfly faerie heard her in his
mind.

"No I do not," he answered aloud.

Ciera smiled at him. "Answer me please in your mind for it
is open to me." Her eyes flitted to either side quickly then she
added, "...he listens, I am sure."

Madrena set down her soup bowl. She had sat close to
Adren, that kind of close you know, that makes a mother wonder. "Who is IBNot, mom?" she asked.

For the next few minutes Ciera told them both of who he
was, the encounters with him and of how through him, Rhetoric knew their every move...so explaining their need to draw
him out. There was a pause, dinner finished and soon the
entire troop sat around a single campfire listening to how
Ciera and Enol planned to do just that. It was dangerous. No
words were spoken aloud, nothing could be heard except the
roaring waters at the sides of their camp, but do not doubt
that someone was listening, even though he heard nothing...

and watched.

Ciera was sure IBNot would show himself, not because he thought it was a smart thing, but because quite frankly Rhetoric wanted Enol dead so his magic would drain from the books, and he could replace it with his own. Rhetoric would be controlling him. His will would not be his. While IBNot is well aware of the fifth day of Venus and its implications she continued, his evil possessor might not be and would not care even if he was. As with the ghost soldier, Anhur, Rhetoric cared nothing for the abominations he created or their death. He would only be able to see the opportunity of killing Enol.

At this, Enol said, "Really? So now, once again, all I am to you is bait?" Her husband turned glancing around at everyone rolling his eyes, a playful look in them. "See? See why she lets me come along!"

Everyone had laughed, except the face that watched, as he could not hear their thoughts. His wife placed a loving hand on the side of his face and Enol touched her arm. A short moment in the knowledge of the love they shared showed in each others' eyes.

Ciera turned back to the others briefly her mouth revealing a small playful smirk of her own that Enol could not see then back toward her husband saying with a smile, "You are correct only in the first part my dear, the bait part." Her smile faded and her tone changed. "But, if we can use Rhetoric's selfish needs while he is linked to IBNot and lure him into the clearing, it is possible that with the dragonfly dagger we could rid our worlds of Rhetoric and IBNot in one shot…maybe."

Different expressions could be seen around the group at the thought of what could happen as Ciera's eyes now turned specifically on Adren, then down at the dagger at his side.

"I see that fortunately there are two, for mine has been lost to Rhetoric."

Ciera patted her own empty sheath.

The young dragonfly faerie smiled at her, raising both his brows in unison.

"If you did not know of the second one, maybe Rhetoric does not either," thought Adren adding, "and who's to say that there is but two."

An eyebrow went up on Enol, his lips parted slightly and he remembered something he had been meaning to mention. He squeezed Ciera's hand, changing the subject by speaking aloud and the ears of IBNot heard.

"Early this morning," he paused, taking a quick breath as a stab of pain from the wound of the talon made him winch. "When your mother and I found Emmit and the other faerie soldiers, I wondered at first why Rhetoric would feel the need to send his soldiers to Whisper Hollow when he was already able to call to the books and they were answering, and disappearing at his request." He paused again, his hand gently rubbing the talon strike.

Sneak, wing now fully healed saw him and spoke up continuing the thought aloud.

"The thirteenth book is what he wants. Maybe when it specifically did not answer he sent them after the trunk, thinking that the thirteenth book would be inside."

Pausing briefly he tapped a finger against his lips and added, "I believe his soldiers were the same ravens we fought earlier." He lowered his eyes to Enol's thigh and winched as well, as though feeling his friend's, his leader's pain by remembering the pain of his own burned wing.

A smile came across the face of IBNot, "Smart boy," it said with a voice not its own.

Ciera had redressed his wound when she arrived with Madrena but a spot of blood could be seen once more. Sneak looked into Enol's eyes, seeing discomfort and continued. "They overpowered six well trained faerie soldiers, I know; I trained with them. He must have sent all of them. That is why we have not had more encounters with those evil birds. They were busy."

Madrena broke in now, "You can rest assured they did not get the trunk and the thirteenth book. Our soldiers did not die in vain. They believed in the power of the books, and in all of us."

Ciera looked with pride at her daughter. Night was right, she did seem stronger, and yes, older.

The eyes and ears that watched and listened from the darkness, unknowing, had the same thought.

Madrena instantly glanced up at her mother shooting her a smile, having heard her thoughts, then looked over at her father, worry in her eyes. He sat quiet, lips pursed as if thinking of all that was being said. She spoke in thought. "Father, do you think Rhetoric knew that the books would come to him with faeries attached?"

"No, I do not," he answered. "But we have gotten away from the reason I mentioned the thirteenth book in the first place." Enol pressed his lips tightly together looking from face to face around the fire then spoke silently to them. "You have all traveled long and hard to protect the books, and to save Madrena." He nodded toward Logren, Maleah and the other elk, "And you, to save your children. We will be successful in the defeat of Rhetoric." He glanced over at his daughter. "The thirteenth book is safe and as long as we follow the plan tomorrow morning we are one step closer to that success!"

The eyes saw the glance, but the ears once more could not hear their thoughts.

Tarin and his group had been sitting quietly, following the trail of thoughts as they had been sent, but now their leader felt the need to speak aloud as well.

"We must rescue the faeries and the books that Rhetoric has taken!"

Enol and Tarin's eyes met, a silent reply was given.

"I agree with you my friend and we will. Knowing these faeries like I do and their capabilities I prefer however to see them not as prisoners and that they need rescuing, but as allies, on the inside."

All heads including Tarin's nodded in agreement.

Now Enol turned toward Madrena. "I think tomorrow my dear, after we have dealt with IBNot we will need a diversion from the inside." He winked at her and she winked back.

Ciera stood, stretching, sending another silent thought out. "Nip and Tuck have reported back and the wall of stone has been located. The Wind Riders will arrive tomorrow morning. They will be our diversion on the outside." She paused, looking back over her shoulder into the dark behind them, and they all heard her wonder about Cinq, Saynk and Sunck.

"They will be here soon. I am sure of it," said Peakin softly as she stood and others stood with her. They were all tired. "We should rest now. Tomorrow will be an eventful day."

The Queen of the Faeries hung her head momentarily then raised it. Today had indeed been in eventful day, but she forced a smile to her face and said aloud.

"Not one of us knows what tomorrow will bring. I just want to say that I am proud to know you all, and mighty glad you are on my side."

"How sweet," said the mouth of IBNot in a voice that once again was not his own.

Sneak was the first to respond, pulling his sword from its sheath, holding it in the air, saying the first, "Hear! Hear!" while everyone else followed in unison.

One by one both faerie and elk started leaving the campfire.

Ciera looked toward her daughter, "We have room in our tent for you my dear."

"Thanks mom, I brought my own tent. I will be fine."

The father look came instantly from Enol, traveling from Madrena to Adren who immediately spoke up.

"I will sleep just outside it. I will protect her with my life."

The look from Enol continued until Ciera tugged at his hand.

"She will be fine. Come, let us rest."

He turned, limping slightly and was the first to enter their tent, concern still showing on his face. Ciera's face however did not show that same concern, and she turned back toward Madrena and Adren before entering.

"Something tells me to be okay with this," she said aloud to them both.

Her eyes softened and she added a silent message to both of them as well as to Tarin, who now walked with his back to them, toward his own group and raised his bow in acknowledgement of it.

* * *

Behind the tree of which he hid, the eyes of IBNot closed, and in his fortress, Rhetoric opened his. The thirteenth book, it must be with them...and where did they have it hidden? ... and who was the man at Madrena's side? His fingers strummed the desk at which he sat loudly and he stared at the book that lay upon it. His book, the Book of Rhetoric, as Madrena had stated.

He pushed the massive desk out, its legs rumbling across the stone and stood walking towards the second of three hallways that led out of the room. No light was needed to follow its winding path. He knew the fortress like he knew the mist.

For just over twenty years now he had been here, imprisoned

by the very mist that he could now control, placed here by Quinn when last he had attempted to control the books. Back then the thirteenth book had been only a rumor, existing only in the bedtime stories of children, but his lengthy stay in the fortress had given him plenty of time to study the past and he had been able to call out to ten of the books through the mist and a certain old man's mind. Yes, he believed most assuredly now, that it did indeed exist.

Rhetoric walked through the open courtyard seeing Anya still wearing the crown, snapping her whip towards the elk attached to spokes that moved the sun wheel, pumping the mist from the depths below. She showed no mercy on them.

One more hallway then down the corridor a few feet and Rhetoric turned pushing open a door to one of the turret rooms. Light invaded the room allowing only feet to be seen on a cot at the other side of it around his massive black striped back and the shadow it shot forth.

"Tell me of the thirteenth book, old man, and who the crown with the thirteen emeralds belongs to!" he thundered.

A small frail hand moved to the eyes of the prisoner on the cot, his eyes squinting from the lack of light and the sudden appearance of it. "You will get no willing help from me," came from him slowly as if every word was a struggle to pronounce. "But know this…true magic never dies."

The voice fell silent and the cape of Rhetoric swirled disturbing the strands of mist below him as he raised his fist angrily walking toward the cot.

"Who is the man with Madrena?" he roared.

The hand fell away from the eyes and the frail man's head fell back upon the cot; a small smile showed upon his face. He said nothing, his weakened condition overcoming him once more as he fell back to sleep. A disgusted look came upon Rhetoric's face as he realized he would get nothing more from the man. He turned fists clenched and stormed from room, slamming the door behind him leaving the man inside in darkness once more. The man's eyes opened and he smiled remembering the second strand of mist that he had seen. Thinking of the allies on the inside Rhetoric himself had brought into his fortress and that it would not be long now.

* * *

Adren stood just outside the tent, its flap slightly open allowing him to keep a watchful eye on Madrena while she slept. He, himself had slept under the stars just briefly, unable to stop thinking of the day to come, and its many possible outcomes. Anything could happen. His hand went to the dagger at his side as he noticed the shimmer of dawn that peaked over the horizon. The morning star would follow. Ciera had asked them, along with Tarin, to meet at their tent shortly before dawn. It was time. Gently he lifted the flap and placed a hand on the shoulder of the woman he now knew, he would forever love.

CHAPTER XIII

The Fifth Day

IT WAS just light enough that they could make out Enol as he sipped his second cup of coffee, sword on his back, ready for the day ahead. Tarin, who was sitting on a rock nearby, was watching him so intently that when Ciera lifted the flap to the tent he nearly fell off in surprise, causing Adren and Madrena to smile as they approached.

Silent good mornings were said and the queen of the faeries quickly ushered them in, all but Enol. She briefly noticed the toweling that served as a bandage on the leg of her husband over the wound from the raven. It was bleeding again. She glanced up into his eyes and mouthed 'I love you' then closed the flap securely.

Quickly, without hesitation and a finger to her mouth signaling silence, Ciera untied the dragonfly dagger and its sheath from around Adren's waist then turned and walked straight over to Tarin.

"Your sheath is needed," she said simply and quietly.

He looked up at her briefly, eyes questioning but his hands wasted no time untying it from his waist, taking his dagger from it and passing it to her. Ciera withdrew the dragonfly dagger from its own sheath, handing it to Tarin and he gazed down, mesmerized by its ornate design.

"Yes, it is quite the eye catcher, is it not?" she said smiling, then continued, "You will need to turn it inside out."

Ciera glanced around the tent at the others who remained silent and whispered, "Rhetoric knows of only one dagger that can kill him. Let's keep it that way."

Gently she slid Adren's dragonfly dagger into Tarin's sheath, folding over the cover to conceal the ornate hilt. It fit perfectly! She returned it to Adren who was smiling broadly.

"I like the way you think Ciera."

She winked at him in response saying, "It is the little things that count, young man." "Agreed!" He answered without hesitation.

The Queen of the faeries smiled then spoke silently to them all. "As you know Logren and his elk sleep with one eye open and our bait stands outside. They will allow IBNot to come as close as possible. I feel he will make his move soon, trying to avoid the morning star's first light."

A clink was heard from outside the tent causing their heads to turn and listen further.

"Dad is probably just putting away his cup and coffee pot Mom," whispered Madrena.

Ciera glanced at her as the second sound was heard, the sound of a sword being drawn. "The first one maybe, but not that one," she responded, grabbing the flap of the tent with one hand and pulling her sword with the other, stepping quickly outside. The others followed, each drawing their swords in succession.

For a second the four stood motionless, mesmerized by the

look of IBNot. Black as the mist, his shape seemed to change as he swung his sword at Enol, arms and legs lengthening and shortening at will. His eyes were empty sockets, and the stink of him engulfed the air around them. The knight magician fought hard, moving toward him, pushing him backward, striking his sword repeatedly, and IBNot fought back just as fiercely.

Ciera saw the black creature glance up to the sky over and over again as he continually lashed out at Enol. He is looking for the morning star she thought.

Dawn was coming fast and Logren and the other elk had moved into place behind IBNot, preventing his retreat. Ciera and the others moved in, closing the circle around them both, and she shot a thought to Enol allowing the others to hear as well.

"Keep him busy just a while longer my husband. He searches for the morning star and it is almost here. Rhetoric cannot be in control of him as of yet."

A loud gurgling sound could be heard and IBNot said, "If I am to die here today, you will come with me!" With that he pushed his free hand deep inside of his own body pulling a dragonfly dagger into full view, Ciera's dagger. He continued swinging his sword in the other, powerfully over and over again, pushing Enol down momentarily on one knee. With both hands the knight magician swung his sword staving off the blows from him, dodging the dagger as it was thrust towards his body.

That's when Ciera saw the change in the eyes of IBNot. Those once empty sockets were now filled with eyes, the eyes of Rhetoric himself.

"Enol!" she yelled, "Rhetoric is within him! His eyes! You must avoid the dagger!"

Again and again the dagger was thrust. On the third thrust

it cut through his sleeve barely missing his arm. It was then that Rhetoric saw his chance as Enol glanced down. He twirled his sword around Enol's sword, catching him off guard, wrenching it from him, tossing it away. There was a short gurgle and the deep voice of Rhetoric spoke.

"You have made it so easy. Now you will die!" The body of IBNot moved closer to him, the dagger high.

Every faerie around had drawn their swords, all ready for whatever might happen, their circle ever shrinking. They must believe! The tiniest twinkle in the northern sky stopped everyone, especially the body of IBNot. It froze, and the eyes of Rhetoric looked down at his useless slave's body.

"My husband will not be dying anytime soon," said Ciera loud enough that Rhetoric heard and he glanced over at her following her pointed finger.

The eyes disappeared instantly, the empty sockets returning. The sparkle of the morning star was the last thing IBNot saw. A gurgling came from his mouth and his body seemed to separate, falling in tiny balls to the earth, flattening; then wriggling like worms into it. The gurgling continued till all were gone. Only the dragonfly dagger remained where it had fallen undamaged to the ground. All the while Rhetoric's angry roar could be heard as he retreated into the mist itself.

Ciera ran to her husband. "The plan was for the bait to win. You had me worried just a little." She smiled, sliding a finger through the cut sleeve. There was no blood. The blade remained virgin.

Enol smiled his half smile, "What? You were worried? ...no worries, under control," and they both laughed and kissed.

It was then that Adren and Sneak walked up to them.

"I believe this is yours," said Adren holding up the dragonfly dagger.

Ciera faced him accepting it from him. "Thank you and

take note that I will be more careful with it in the future." She nodded in gratitude at them both then kissed Enol's cheek sliding the dagger into her sheath as she did.

Peakin and her daughter walked up then, side by side, both with the face of someone who has something up their sleeve. Ciera cocked her head slightly, "Madrena?" she asked. With eyes sparkling, her daughter and Peakin parted without answering, revealing Cinq, Saynk and Sunck. Hugs and handshakes came from all with questions of 'how are you?' and a 'does that hurt?' to Cinq, who still had a small crack on her cheek. All were quiet as Sneakin stepped forward hugging her and all cheered when he kissed her long and deeply, showing his love.

Saynk stepped forward saying with a smile, "It is about time you two!" His attention then turned to Enol. "It is the fifth day, where do you need us?"

The answer was short. "How are you guys with salt water?"

Another smile came from the oldest of the water faeries, "Its water, just taste bad."

Enol placed an open hand on Saynk's shoulder, turning him to go while nodding towards Cinq and Sunck to follow. He stopped in front of Ciera.

"Two questions, my love…are Nip and Tuck awake? …and you, Madrena and Adren are in charge of the diversion inside. Have you come up with any ideas?"

Ciera tapped on her heart twice and a furry head popped up on her left shoulder from behind. It was Nip, bright eyed and ready for the day. Tuck crawled yawning from beneath the shawl, clinging to the strap that held her sheath and dagger. Enol placed a gentle hand under him and Tuck reluctantly jumped in, then he did the same for Nip, who nearly overshot his hand in excitement..

"I guess you can tell who is the morning person between the two," said Ciera, laughing.

Enol held them up at eye level. "Wake up sleepy head," he said, poking Tuck gently. "Both of you are needed today. Your braveness precedes you in tale, so please don't let us down." He smiled down at them as Tuck rubbed his eyes. "We must set up to cross the wall so as not to waste time when the morning mist clears. Your job of finding the wall was crucial to our success…thanks. It is time to show us where it is." A small chirp was heard from each and they scurried off as he knelt, setting them on the ground.

Saynk volunteered, "We will mark the spot," with a wave to his brother and sister.

Enol rose. His wife was ready with her answer to the second question.

"The Wind Riders should arrive shortly my husband and yes, we have ideas." Ciera turned looking at Madrena and Adren. "I think we all know what each other are capable of now, and if a diversion is what you want, it is what you will get."

Enol squeezed her hand. "Call me when the Wind Riders arrive!" He then turned to Adren, whose eyes he met instantly. "If you truly love my daughter you will give your life for her if necessary."

"I do and I would, sir." Their eyes held the stare for a moment more.

He turned then to Madrena saying, "The rest of the day will move very fast my dear." Her father tucked a stray hair behind her ear, "I just want you to know how much you are loved."

She kissed him gently on the cheek. "I will be careful Dad and you as well." He lightly touched her nose and was off.

* * *

It had been decided that Madrena would concentrate on Day, thinking of the turrets at the same time so as to get a visual of where she and the others were being kept. Ciera had remembered seeing a light far down in one of the turrets as she had been carried over by the ravens. Was it the second one? She was sure it was. It must have been Day. It had to be her. The turret room that Ciera herself had been held in had no light. The only light had come from the hallway when Rhetoric had opened the door. It stood to reason it was Day lighting up the turret room where they were being imprisoned.

So Madrena concentrated on the smallest faerie in Whisper Hollow and once more she immediately felt the coolness on her feet of the stone in Rhetoric's fortress. It was so dark! She waited for her eyes to adjust to the only light offered by a single star far above. Staring upward at the top of the turret, she slowly lowered her eyes till shapes starting taking form. What she saw made her gasp and her mouth open wide. Turning in a circle, she counted twenty three faeries shackled to the wall as her mother had been by the black mist. They were talking of the mist and how to break its chain. Madrena smiled as she listened to them. Proud of how they had figured out they were bound by the strand of mist that trailed from under the door. "They are indeed our allies on the inside father," she thought silently, wishing she could let them know she was here and would be back.

Ten books were stacked in the center, it did not surprise her, "…for they are of no use to you Rhetoric unless you kill my father, and that's not going to happen!" she said.

Something flitted through the single stars' light, casting shadows on the floor, causing her to look up as several of Rhetoric's soldiers, the ravens, flew over. There were so many! She said aloud, "I will return my friends," and Madrena closed her eyes, finding herself in front of her mother and Adren again. She grabbed their arms, turning them and pointed out above the mist. "Prepare! The ravens return!"

Ciera yelled for Enol as she ran toward the edge of the black mist where he and the others had lined up to cross the rock wall that separated the Tube and Zacarra. She pointed above the mist and Rhetorics fortress. That was when they heard the first screech from Cedrick. He swooped down close, screeching a greeting at them both but stopped mid sentence listening to Ciera about the ravens. Without question back up he went, screeching a charge order to a large pack of birds that suddenly seemed to come from nowhere and everywhere.

The wind came up suddenly, whipping at their hair and Enol talked loudly, asking, "Who are they?" nodding towards the birds that followed Cedrick.

Ciera smiled and the corner of her eyes crinkled as she squinted into the morning sky. "They are the albatross, and their leader Karnan."

Both of them felt the breeze come up again but could not stop watching as the huge birds swung out over the mist on a direct course for the mass of ravens. Ciera felt a tug on her shawl and looked down to find Maurie.

"My father is here," she said simply and as if finishing her sentence the breeze added, "What is it that you wish of us Ciera?" A strong gust of wind flew by them and the face of Maran could be seen briefly, riding it.

"Clear the air, my friend! Lift the mist from Rhetorics fortress and the waters surrounding it!" she answered.

"The mist is within the water, and is weighted down by it. Only the top of it seems disturbed by our wind," the air filled face said.

Ciera did not hesitate as she looked down at Maurie. "The wind inside of you is needed once more. While your father stirs the mist above, you must lift it from the rock wall sending it up to him. Can you do that?" The small green faerie looked up at her, eyes full of the same wind Ciera had seen at the Forest of Fire. Just how much wind do you have in there little one, passed through her mind as she watched it blow behind the blueness.

"Yes, my queen, I believe I can."

Ciera looked up at Maran, "As you said last time we met, your daughter has a destiny. She will disturb the bottom sending it up to you."

He did not answer immediately but you clearly saw his eyebrow go up as he turned to his daughter smiling. "I knew you had some of your old man inside you!"

He winked at her, and Ciera added, "More than you think!"

Maurie looked to Enol now, asking, "Is everyone ready?"

He did not answer immediately. He was looking up at Cedrick and the albatross, watching along with everyone else as they collided in combat with Rhetorics' ravens, and a mid-air battle of beaks and talons began.

Maran looked down at Maurie tickling her chin with an air filled finger then turned to Enol while nodding toward the battling birds. "We had best get as far as we can while they are being kept occupied."

Enol nodded back in agreement, his jaw was set. "Yes, you are right." He turned to Maurie, who said nothing. She ran quickly, positioning herself out in front of the ones that must cross the wall…of the ones that could not fly.

Enol looked back toward the others briefly, then to Ciera filling her eyes with the love he had for her.

"Be careful!" his wife said as she touched his lips with her thumb slightly moving it across them both. "The rock walls of Rhetorics fortress crumble easily. They are impregnated with the mist, weakened by it I think, which could be useful." Her hand now slipped to the side of his face.

"You be careful too, my love. See you on the inside!" he said back softly.

Enol stared at her for a moment longer then raised his hand in the air, signaling Maurie to lead them on. He mouthed, "I love you," and ran to lead the others just behind the small green faerie that would, with the help of her father, clear the way for them to Rhetoric's fortress.

Ciera filled his head with, "Me, too."

He saw her turn, running back towards Madrena and Adren and saw the three of them grasp hands. He also saw Madrena wink at him and heard Ciera say in his head, "Remember Anya, she hides at the gate!" and they were gone!

Enol thought of the thirteenth book, marveling at the power it had bestowed on his daughter. What was it she had told him, yes, that her and the book were one.

The knight magician turned, looking to the skies. Cedrick and the Albatross seemed to be holding their own. There were so many ravens though. He felt a tug on his sleeve and looked down at Maurie and her windy blue eyes.

"Yes, it is time my dear,"

The small faerie leaped up on the nearest boulder closest to the mist at the spot Nip and Tuck had marked as the beginning of the rock wall. With her webbed feet firm against it she opened her mouth allowing the wind within her to escape.

At first the mist did not seem to want to move, but as her father Maran and the other two Wind Riders started moving the top...it did. Slowly but surely a top chunk of the mist broke away, swirling in front of them, then spiraling up and out allowing them to see the rock wall they must cross on for the first time. It was about nine feet wide at its widest and a mere path at its smallest. Deep crevices had formed along the sides over time as the waves of both rivers continually beat down upon it. Water splashed up and over the wall continually, reminding all of the constant threat of being swept off into the raging waves.

Cinq and Sunck flew over towards the salty water of the Zacarra while Saynk flew towards the fresh water of the Tube saying, "This is where we come in!"

With wings spread wide, all three hovered between the waves and the rock wall, protecting them from their crashing blows as all took their first steps onto the rock wall.

Enol was right behind Maurie, stopping only briefly to pick up Nip and Tuck, who waited at the waters edge, followed by Tarin and his group, and Sneakin and Peakin.

It had been prearranged that Logren would carry Id and Odd across on the log that held them firmly in his mouth, while his wife Maleah and the other elk took up the rear.

All the while Maurie blew the mist up and the Wind Riders lifted it little by little, taking it away, allowing the blue morning sky to show through. From time to time they caught sight of the birds and their battle above. At one point, an albatross fell from the sky above, landing on the rock wall in front of them, instantly swept away by the waves; then a raven…and another and another. All were at one point knocked to their knees by the endless onslaught of water. One elk was lost to the Zacarra, as was one of the Amberwood faeries. Sunck had tried to catch him, but instantly Bramer had been sucked under.

Enol wiped wet hair out of his eyes, looking forwards then backwards to check on the others. He watched as Sneakin caught one, then another of the Amberwood faeries as they too were nearly swept away. They must get through. They must make it to Rhetorics. Their faerie friends, the elk's children, and Madrena, Ciera, and Adren were depending on them to do just that. He pulled his sword, pausing just long enough as he struggled to raise it through the almost endless spray of water and said, "This way my friends, we are almost there!" …and they were.

* * *

It had been a first for Ciera. She was amazed at her daughter's powers, the thirteenth books' power, and the abilities she now possessed because of it. Never before had she arrived at her destination so quickly…and in the flesh. Madrena had brought them all here instantly just by remembering. What had she said? …oh, yes. All she had to do was remember the page in the book.

As their eyes adjusted to the darkness, a faint glow started on the other side of the turret room. It was Day. Light flooded the room and a voice Madrena knew well spoke up from behind.

"It's about time you got here." It was Fire. She turned and ran toward him throwing her arms around his neck, squeezing him tightly with closed eyes.

"Happy to see you too!" he said laughing.

Madrena's eyes opened and she gave him a last squeeze. She stood back, eyebrow up, lips curved in that mischievous grin they all knew so well. "You could at least give me a hug back."

"My princess, if I could I…" Fire stopped mid sentence, for the first time feeling the freedom of his wrists. "How did you do that?" he asked.

"Seems that nasty mist does not like me, mmmh, mmmh… nope!" she answered, her eyes sparkling like her mothers' could.

Night was the first to catch on. "Where's my hug?"

Madrena turned, showing a huge smile on her face.

"On its way!" she said walking across the room, pointing

and adding to the others, "You're next!" passing the stack of books in the center of the turret room.

She stopped in front of Night giving him a wink and placed both her hands on his tiny upper arms and the mist shrunk up and away from her. It did not break its hold on the others however. Reuniting just above where Night had been held as it had with Fire, it kept the rest of them shackled to the wall, but Night was free and Madrena kissed him on his small cheek.

He responded, "Better than a hug any day!" and flew over landing on the ten books in the center of the room, rubbing his wrists and ankles, glad to be free of the crawling mist.

Ciera had moved over next to the door and was now motioning to her daughter. "Madrena if you can break the chain of mist here then maybe you could free them all at once."

"Good idea," added Adren who had been counting the faeries held captive. There were twenty three, twenty three more to aid in the defeat of Rhetoric.

"You are right Mom but first things first," Madrena said holding up a finger and turning to the books. "Excuse me Night." He flew upward hovering just at her side and she picked up five up them and was gone. She reappeared briefly picking up the other five and disappeared again.

Night, Fire and the other faeries watched in amazement. They had never seen these powers. Never known their princess possessed them. 'But how's' could be heard around the room and Ciera placed a finger to her mouth sending the thought of "Rhetoric could be listening."

Madrena appeared and she looked to Adren then to her mother answering the question she could see on their face. "They are in the cave," as she walked to the door. All watched the mist move up the crack of the doorway, anticipating her, avoiding her. She smiled, watching it position itself at the top of the doorway, just out of hands reach.

"You cannot escape me."

She unfolded her wings, spreading them wide. This turret room was much larger than the one her mother had been held in. Had they wanted to they could all fly out through the top of it, but that was not the plan. A diversion was needed on the inside to allow her father and the others time to enter Rhetoric's fortress.

"I am not sure exactly how this will work," she said, glancing back around the room. "You had better be ready for anything!"

Madrena moved toward the door covering it from top to bottom with her body and wings. The mist jumped away instantly splitting in two, one end disappearing outside the door, the other lashing upward like the second half of a worm split in two, knowing it is dying, but still wriggling with its last breaths. Stepping back from the door she refolded her wings, watching as the mist on the wall squirmed and snapped its cut end.

Suddenly it raced up the turret wall showing no signs of stopping, jerking up the other twenty one faeries still held in its grip with it. Adren was quick to react. Dropping the swords he had carried for Smoke, Fire and Piggett, he grabbed Madrena by the waist saying, "Hold on!" He flew upward so fast the passing faeries seemed a blur.

Her presence was all that was needed. One by one the mist let go of its captives as each was passed, sending them wings spread to the floor below with Ciera and the others. The last three, including Day, were released just at the top of the turret as the mist shot off into the now blue sky above, only to be whisked away by the blowing winds of the Wind Riders. Adren and Madrena descended back to the turret floor to a room full of smiles.

Ciera was first to speak. "The mist has retreated to its owner." She glanced Madrena's way. "That means Rhetoric will be here as he was before." She noticed the faeries as they rubbed the black marks left on their wrist and ankles by the mist. "Don't worry, my sister said it only sticks to evil and she would know."

"Rhetoric must be covered in the stuff then," said Adren as he handed Smoke, Fire and Piggett their swords, then opened the door allowing light to flood the room, adding, "Time to go."

Madrena moved to his side now, placing her hand in his. "Everyone this is Adren. If you have not guessed he is on our side."

Nods came from all as Ciera said, "Day."

"Yes?" she answered, her light turned down now that the light from the hall filled the room.

"We will need your light again. How are you?"

The blond faerie of no more than ten inches smiled and answered, "I'm good!"

Her queen nodded with a smile as she pulled both Night's and her sword from the pouch on her side. Each of the small faeries in turn took their sword, replacing it in the sheaths they still wore on their backs as Ciera continued. "Night, you and Fire will stay with us. Day, you and the others must find the elk that are prisoners here as well and free them."

"Elk?" replied Day instantly.

Adren spoke up now, smiling at the tiny faerie, saying, "I imagine they are being kept in an inner courtyard my small new friend. I believe you will find them if you concentrate on the hallways to the left. Their parents are outside the fortress walls with Enol and are huge. I do not think these turret rooms would hold their children, and as with you, they were brought here for a reason."

Ciera, who was watching just outside the door for Rhetoric, turned and added, "Find them, free them, and storm them through his fortress toward the front gates. Enol will be waiting to enter. Then, take you and them to safely across the rock wall."

Piggett objected immediately. "But my queen, there are many of us and safety for all is in numbers."

Ciera's eyes softened as she scanned all the faces of the faeries in front of her. "The books, your books, are safe. If for some reason we fail," she paused and Adren quickly piped in, "...And we will not!"

Ciera smiled, continuing, "...if for some reason we do, you all will be free to carry on." She once again paused, glancing back at Adren, "But of course, we will always believe."

She had barely finished her sentence when a loud thud was heard from above, followed by a short swooshing sound and two more thuds, as one of the larger ravens skidded down the inner turret walls and landed on the floor, directly behind them.

"Oh yeah," Ciera added as all eyes stared at its mangled body. "Watch out for the ravens."

Piggett and Smoke pulled their swords while the rest of them stood still staring down at the huge bird. "Just in case," says Piggett aloud.

Day nodded in agreement, her dagger now ready as well. The raven was at least one hundred times her size. She waved at the others signaling them to follow and they left silently down the hall disappearing to the right.

Now Ciera turned to Fire and Night. She saw the red glow of Fire's eyes and smiled. "I am glad to see you are feeling better."

His lips curled into a small smile, "My heat is at your

disposal, but it does not affect the mist. We tried it."

"It is not the mist but the vines within the turret walls that must burn, my friend." Madrena smiled at what her mother had said. "More diversion…I like it!"

"Yes," agreed Adren adding, "I will find Rhetoric and keep him busy till Enol can get through the gate."

Ciera objected immediately, glancing to Madrena then back at him.

"No, Night and I will find him and my sister. You go with Madrena and Fire. Check every turret room for other prisoners, then Fire you do your thing."

She placed a hand on Adren's shoulder. "You have said that Madrena is your destiny, not to mention that we both carry a dragonfly dagger which is better off in two different places. Yours is the reserve."

"You are brave Ciera," he nodded slowly. "Do not hesitate to call out. We will be there."

The Queen of the Faeries smiled at him. "Do not worry, I will."

The mood was lightened by Night who now stood on Madrena's shoulder and said chuckling, "Fire, I think that we are way behind in this adventure and that stories around the fire in the future are gonna be doozies!"

Smiles came from all then Ciera pulled her sword. "I think I agree with Piggett!" she said more seriously, stepping through the doorway to peer down the hall adding, "Everyone is careful, understand!"

"And you as well my mother," said Madrena from behind her as she stepped into the corridor.

Adren followed turning back to Fire, "Might as well start with this one," he said nodding toward the now empty turret room.

Fire smiled, walking into the room that had kept himself

and his fellow faeries captive with the mist. "My pleasure!" he responded. Adren watched amazed at the heat the faerie named Fire could generate as he merely walked around the room and the vines ignited. In seconds he stepped back through the doorway saying, "Next?" as the flames barreled up the turret walls behind him.

"Impressive," remarked Adren as they all started down the corridor towards the next room, wondering who else Rhetoric had locked in his fortress.

* * *

The chain of mist had once more retreated forcefully to Rhetoric, but this time he had heard it coming, catching it with an open hand and casting it over his shoulder. It sank into his skin like it had been there all along, creating yet another stripe down his back.

He growled. Quinn had cursed him with this blackness, this mist, but he had learned to control it and use it. No one had ever broken free of it, until Ciera.

He turned to Anya who stood beside him at the front gate then towards the carcasses of both ravens and albatross that littered the courtyard. More of them were ravens.

Anya looked down at the last chain of mist that wove its way from him and into the fortress walls. "Who has escaped?"

Rhetoric stared down at the last chain, his eyes angered slits. He did not answer her question but asked instead with a snarling voice. "Who and how many stand outside?"

Anya spit in her hand, rubbing the black spittle on the wall. Her powers of sight had been frozen by her father but she too had learned to cope with the mist somewhat. With IBNot dead and gone she was his only option to see what was indeed beyond the gate and she liked that he must rely on her.

The picture that formed on the wall was blurred but showed the outline of Enol instantly, and Rhetoric growled again. "You will not win this time!" He glared at the image until Anya pointed out the blueness behind the images and his question of how many was temporarily forgotten. "The mist!" he roared looking up. Swirls of blue could be seen beyond the still battling birds. Rhetoric spun around. "Go and check the elk! They must pump harder!" She nodded, ducking back through the arches and into the inner walls of the fortress and was gone.

The blackened figure looked down at his hands and arms. The mist still moved but it had slowed, and the true stripes of the curse were now showing more vividly. Without the constant flow of mist he would not be able to shoot it; his chances to defeat Enol and the others would lessen. His minds' eye saw the box in his room and he too disappeared into the inner walls of the fortress.

* * *

Madrena, Adren and Fire had searched all but one of the turrets now, finding no one inside them. The vines inside the turrets had been thick and the flames that Fire created burned brightly as they chased each other up the turret walls. It had felt good to see the room that had held her mother burn thought Madrena.

On ahead in the hallway, they could see the flames of the first turret room they had burned still licking through the doorway. They had come full circle, the inner castle at their backs now as they stood in front of the last door. Something was different though, a strand of mist flowed under it and Madrena stamped down on it with her foot before it could jump away sending the broken end like a sling shot down the hall, some of it into the stone as before and the other end under the door. She looked up at Adren and over to Fire, their thoughts one. Someone was most definitely imprisoned in this room. Adren stepped in front of Madrena, opening the door, and like the other turret rooms light invaded the darkness within.

* * *

A small window was the only source of light in the room with the blackened walls where Rhetoric stood. His hands held the box he had hidden for many years, waiting for this very moment. Gently he lifted the lid revealing the ornate dagger with the equally ornate sheath, quickly pulling it out, letting the box fall to the floor and strapped it on his waist.

* * *

It had been the third hallway to the left that Day and the others had taken. It was the first one that light could barely be seen down, building the hope of an inner courtyard. One by one they went through the darkened hallway. The stone floor was uneven. Many of the stones' corners pointed upwards in spots to trip up the unaware so Day flew at their feet, offering the all seeing light she could. Thin lines of mist could be seen in the cracks of the stones on the wall and the floor but it did not move. Skinnie, who took up the rear stopped.

His brother Hyde whispering loudly, "Come on, keep up!" But Skinnie did not move, and Day hearing them and knowing the need for quiet, turned bringing her light to the spot where he stood.

He pointed at the walls and the mist whispering, "It is not moving anymore."

"Yes, you are right, it is not," she agreed.

Her eyes looked up and down the rock wall. Each crack held the same line of non moving mist and the lines seemed thinner, all but one and it moved slowly back the way they had come. She smiled looking back at the faeries pointing the way they were headed. "Ladies and Gentlemen, I think this is a main passageway for the mist to get to the outer portions of the castle. Meaning it comes from somewhere ahead. We must hurry!" She patted Skinnie on the shoulder, "Good catch!" and flew forward once more offering the much needed light at their feet holding her dagger in a ready position.

Moments later they broke into the open courtyard, crowding the doorway in silence, each one frozen, some of their eyes filling with tears at what they saw. Seven elk, some standing some lying down in pure exhaustion were harnessed to a huge wooden wheel…a sun wheel of sorts. Scars from the leather that bound them could be seen on their chest and around their necks. A striped woman stood yelling with a whip in hand, lashing out at them repeatedly, trying to get them to move. The same woman who had helped Rhetoric chain them to the wall with the mist.

Three strands of mist wove their way upward from the center of the sun wheel that held the elk to the now blue skies above and they were getting thinner by the moment. That wheel must pump it, pump it straight up from below; and these elk were its power source thought Day. "Move away from them!" she shouted as the light within her faded.

The figure stiffened, turning slowly, showing the face and features they knew as their queens' but it was not…it was Anya. "I do not take orders from you little one," she answered, lashing her whip out once more toward the elk closest to her, cutting its left flank with the barbed end.

Day stood on Piggett's shoulder, her jaw set. "Maybe not, but we are here to free those elk and you will not stop us."

Anya smiled and the faeries cringed. This woman may look like their queen, even be her sister but she was indeed not. Her teeth and tongue had been blackened by the mist, her hair hung in black clumps gnarled at the roots under the crown she wore. The very way she held herself showed them that she was not queen material.

"Which one of you will fight me first?" she said, dropping the whip, pulling her sword then sneering at Day, "You little one?"

With no hesitation Smoke placed a hand on Piggett's other shoulder and stepped in front of them. "I will," he stated firmly.

Day flew to his shoulder immediately. "We will fight her together!" she whispered.

He smiled at her with one side of his mouth, "I will keep her busy. You free the elk." Day looked at the others, mouth pinched, then back at him, directly in his eyes. "No heroics. Just keep her busy. If she is half as good with that sword as our queen, you're in trouble."

Anya spoke up from across the room. "I heard that and I am better than my goody two shoes sister…any day."

"We'll see about that," replied Smoke, stepping towards her, sword high. The first swing of her sword surprised him some what. She was strong, very strong. There would be no just keeping her busy. This would be the fight of his life. He swung back defiantly over and over again, each time remembering the one word he and the others had been taught all their lives… Believe!…while Day and the others cut the leather straps that imprisoned the elk.

Anya was good, staving off his blows repeatedly as she backed her way toward the only other hallway that led out of the courtyard. She had noticed that the elk were now free and knowing she was outnumbered had chosen retreat. Her eyes met Smoke's and she said with the snarl of something truly evil, "We're through here." Lashing out yet again with her sword she caught his at the hilt, pulling it from his grasp, flinging it across the room at Hyde's feet, then brought it back around fast to meet its mark in Smoke's chest. Anya glared at him, then at the others, defiantly pulling the sword from his wound. Smiling as he limply fell to the floor and she stepped backward into the hallway, disappearing, encased immediately in the darkness it held.

Hyde was the first at his side, Smoke's sword in hand. "Hold on Smoke," he said gently.

Piggett was beside himself. He peered down the hallway saying loudly, "We should go after her!"

Day held out her hand offering her wrap as a bandage and Hyde took it placing it on the wound pressing hard to stop the bleeding. She flew over to the enraged Piggett.

"Our first duty is to our queen and her orders, my friend." Day turned, catching the eyes of Hyde's, Skinny's and the other faeries of Whisper Hollow then turned back to him. "But we all agree and wish we could follow."

Piggett looked over at his friends seeing the same worry and anger he himself felt and thought of the elk, and the order to storm them through the fortress once they were free. His eyes centered on the elk and he asked aloud, "Which of you is the strongest?"

The largest of them walked from around the wooden wheel. Scars covered his body, more so than the others. "I am," he said.

Together the faeries placed their friend on his back. Piggett picked up the leather straps from the floor they had just cut off from under the wooden wheel and placed a hand on the shoulder of huge elk.

"I am sorry but I must once again place these around you. I am afraid my friend will not be able to hold on."

"Do what you must," was the great elk's answer.

As Piggett tied Smoke to the elk Day pointed down the hallway Anya disappeared down, her light bright once more. "We know where the other hallway leads. This one must lead towards the front of the fortress. I will lead the way, you elk follow, and faeries of Whisper Hollow guard our backs!" She now turned her attention fully to the elk and added, "Others wait outside the gate to defeat Rhetoric and Anya. You my friends are needed to open that gate."

The elk that held their friend answered her with his first reason to smile in a long time, "How fast can you fly little one?"

"Fast enough," Day smiled back quickly and off they all shot into the hallway. Day's light beaming brightly, illuminating the hall for the elk stampeding behind her, and the faeries of Whisper Hollow that were hot on their heels.

* * *

Immediate tears had formed in Madrena's eyes at the sight of the man that lay on the cot on the other side of the turret room. He was frail. His long thinned gray hair and beard almost covered his even thinner body. It was her grandfather in the flesh.

"We thought you were dead, gone with Quiviera," she sobbed, hugging him as he shaded his eyes from the light of the hallway with one hand and placed the other lightly on her cheek.

"Nothing matters, you have found me." His voice was forced and raspy.

Adren stepped forward now placing his own hand on Quinn's shoulder. He remembered the man in Quiviera just two days before and how healthy he had looked. It must have taken almost everything he had left to create the image. "I think your daughter Ciera had a hunch we would find you here. We must go. I will carry you."

Madrena stood taking Fire's place at the door, tears still in her eyes remembering the two strands of mist that had hung behind Rhetoric the first time they had met in the turret room where her mother had been held. "Burn this room even more than the others Fire. Send a message to Rhetoric."

* * *

Enol and the others stood just outside the gate now. All swords were drawn. All eyes alert to the threat of the birds above, to their death dives, and to what might come through the huge gate that closed them out of Rhetorics' fortress.

Sneakin walked up placing a hand on his shoulder. "So what do you think that queen of ours is stirring up in there?" he said smiling.

"Trouble most likely!" responded Enol quickly, a smile filling his face.

They had gathered just outside the gate, Anya had not shown herself. Id, Odd and Nip and Tuck had been over the area twice now, and not found a trace of her.

The area was small and with the elk, well room was sparse, making it that much easier to get hit by the falling birds. However, the skies were clearing and Cedrick, Karnan and the albatross seemed to have the ravens under control, the bulk of them were now dead or had deserted. Only a few thin slivers of black mist trailed through the sky. They seemed connected and they seemed to have common roots in the fortress itself.

Enol pushed on the huge gate. It was nearly three times as tall as he. It barely moved.

"I cannot wait much longer Sneak," he stated catching Logren's eye and shooting in thought, "We need to talk my friend." The huge elk walked up and Enol sized him up to the door, nodding at it. "Do you think you could open that?"

Logren placed his rack up against the door and pushed steadily. Groaning and creaking could be heard. The hinges seemed to bend at his power.

Suddenly he stepped back, cocking his head. Enol's eye twitched.

"Do you hear that?" asked the great elk.

The knight magician leaned forward. He did hear something. Turning, he raised his hand sending out a thought to all who waited behind him. "Please, quiet...please," and there was silence.

Enol placed his ear directly to the door. Yes, he could hear something and it was getting louder! Quickly he turned to them again, no thought was sent this time, he yelled. "Get back! Everyone move back away from the door!"

* * *

Ciera and Night had searched every corridor they had come to, but no sight of Rhetoric or Anya had been seen. The room they were in now was larger than any other room they had encountered, a single massive desk sat in its center, the book of Rhetoric laying open on top. The only other piece of furniture was a chair that was pushed out and away from it.

Ciera whispered over to Night. "Not much on decorating, are they."

He smiled back at her pointing at the puddle that stood at the base of the desk and he flew down, standing next to it. "Mist..."

Ciera walked over standing motionless above it.

"Mist that no longer moves," she added, her eyebrow moving upward.

He answered quickly, "That can only be good!" as he rubbed his wrists remembering the burn and itch of its touch.

Suddenly their eyes met, each one knowing the other had

felt it. The stones beneath their feet had rumbled, just barely then they heard a voice from behind say, "You will all pay for what you have done here."

Night stood motionless at the base of the desk. It was the mist that slowly moved up the legs that caught his eyes first, striping the man who had spoken. It was Rhetoric. "Could he see him," he thought?

His queen heard his thoughts and shot back an "I'm not sure" then quickly said aloud to Rhetoric, changing the subject, "I see you have been studying your book."

She glanced quickly at it then back towards him, reliving in her mind the earlier up close encounter with the mist he could shoot, knowing well she should beware.

He answer was short, his voice now clearer than it had been back in the turret room where he had almost gurgled, speaking through mist that had then welled up in his throat.

"There is nothing in it. It is empty." He too then glanced at the book, but his eyes returned to her just as quickly, thinking about the mist as well and his questionable ability to shoot it. It felt different now, the way it moved on his body had slowed. It seemed to weigh him down. Ciera tried to read his thoughts but could not. A gleam of metal came from his side but her vision of what was there was obscured in the dim light of the room. She continued by saying, "As with any book the pages are empty until they are written."

That was when the pages of the book on the table started to glow. Even Night could see the glow from beneath the table. What he could not see was the writing that appeared. The words were old world, not recognizable to either Rhetoric or Ciera. The pages flipped and more writing appeared that neither could read. Both of them were frozen, mesmerized by the book and what it was doing.

It was the loud rumble that broke their stares, causing them all to look up and over at a small light coming fast toward them, up the hallway across the room. The rumble grew louder and louder, shaking the stones they stood on causing even Rhetoric to steady himself as Day, the elk and the other faeries thundered through and right back into another hallway straight across the room.

Ciera smiled as she heard Night yell at his sister, "Found, freed and storming! Way to go, sis!" Her thoughts returned to Rhetoric and she turned quickly around to find him gone and he had the book.

The sound of splintering wood alongside a series of thuds could be heard down the hallway and Night yelled, "The gate! They must have gone right through it!"

Off he flew with Ciera right behind him.

* * *

The hallway was a short one. Day could see the gate ahead as they went through it and into the outer courtyard. She flew up and back down landing on Smoke's upper chest just as the huge elk barreled through the gate, breaking the hinges and splintering the wooden cross bar that had kept Enol and the others from entering. Cheers, snorts, and the pounding of hooves could be heard as they broke through.

Day flew instantly to Enol's shoulder as they ran by.

"Sorry, we would have been here sooner but we did not hear you knock!"

She smiled but then her face turned serious as they turned to Smoke.

"Anya."

Enol walked over to him, laying his hand on the young faeries arm. "How are you doing my friend?"

"Still breathing sir, too stubborn to stop I guess," he answered slowly, forcing a weak smile.

Enol patted his arm, "You keep that up, okay?"

* * *

Dark cubbies filled the corridors that wound their way throughout the fortress and Anya knew them all. She had run down
the hall darting into one of them, hiding in the dark just out
of sight of Day, the elk and the other faeries as they ran past
until she heard Madrena's voice. She made her way back towards
the room where the elk had been enslaved, hiding behind the
wooden wheel and its spokes.

* * *

The turret room had ignited instantly. The flames created by
Fire had spread upward in a rage, as if he himself felt the pain
of their mentor Quinn having been imprisoned there for so
many years. They stood there briefly watching, Adren holding
the frail man in his arms. That was when they felt the rumble
and heard a thundering noise too.

"The elk!" exclaimed Madrena, "Day and the others…they
must have found them!"

All three turned and raced up the hallways to the source of
the sound and entered the inner courtyard. Dust from the
hooves of the elk still filled the room but sunlight shone
through from the sky above.

Quinn was the first to speak as he lifted his arm and pointed
at the spokes and the sun wheel they had been attached to. "It
is the source of the mist. Rhetoric must have made a deal with
the devil himself."

"And the elk were needed to pump it up," added Adren,
noticing the straps under the spokes.

Their attention was suddenly drawn to the hallway across
the room when a loud, crashing sound was heard. It had to be
the front gate.

Adren lowered his eyes to Quinn. "Are you well enough to stand?"

"I believe so," he answered.

Madrena watched as Adren gently set him down, seeing once again his frailty.

She turned to Fire, "From the tracks on the floor and the dust in the air, my friend; Day, the others and the elk went down that hallway," she paused nodding toward it. "Please take my grandfather out to my father, who should be entering the fortress now."

"But my princess," objected Fire.

Madrena placed a finger to his lips. "I will be fine. I am depending on you to get him to safety."

He sighed, knowing full well she was right and that Quinn could not withstand any sort of confrontation in his condition. "Yes, my princess. It shall be done."

Reluctantly Fire started down the hallway, supporting Quinn as they moved down the hall, his red eyes lighting the way. It curved to the right and as the light from the open courtyard disappeared from behind, another light in front of them illuminated the room ahead. Fire looked down at Quinn, the old man was pale, his shoulders hunched. Madrena was right. He must get him out of this place.

Something moved in the light ahead, causing him to look up. A shadow stood at the entry of the room. Fire smiled, it was Enol, who immediately ran towards them. Their eyes met.

"My daughter and Adren are they with," he stopped mid sentence seeing the man Fire supported. "Quinn, is that you?"

The old man lifted his head slightly, able to barely nod in ascent. Enol grabbed the other side of him and they walked into the room with the massive desk, sitting him in the chair as Ciera ran to his side. She traced his face with her fingertips.

"I knew that dream was too real to ignore. You are safe now."

Sneakin and Peakin, who were guarding the hallway across the room stood mouths open at the sight of Quinn, moving only when they heard Enol call them over.

"Take him to the other side…protect him. If for some reason we fail, he must survive." Enol did not wait for a reply, he then turned to Fire, "Your brother has been hurt…go to him."

Fire stared into to his eyes and Enol read his thoughts…he was torn between duty and his brother. "Family is what counts. That is why we are all ultimately here. Now go…be with Smoke." Fire held the stare a moment longer, pursing his lips, finally agreeing with a nod.

Sneakin and Peakin carefully helped Quinn to his feet but before they could turn to go their mentor raised his hand. He held his head up as best as he could.

"The book of Rhetoric, it is a key," his voice was weak and both Ciera and Enol had to come closer to him to hear.

"A key, father?" his daughter asked.

"Yes a key, a key that can seal any exit or any cell."

His head bobbed, his strength was waning. "You must find Madrena," another bob.

"She must command the book! She alone must read the ligature."

He now slumped slightly forward in pure exhaustion. Ciera kissed his forehead and said to Sneakin and Peakin, "Please get him back across that wall. Take care of him and yourselves."

Both nodded and then turned to Enol who added, "Have Logren and three of the biggest elk stay behind and be ready, ready for anything."

The two of them watched as the four of them left through the hallway that led to the gate and freedom. Ciera turned placing a hand to her husband's face.

"I need a kiss."

Enol smiled, giving it to her easily. She kissed him back then turned his face towards the hallway Fire and her father had come out of with the hand still on his face.

"I think our destiny is down that hallway."

He responded with an "mmhh" and nodded then cocked his head a little sideways at her.

"What is this ligature that our daughter must read?"

Ciera looked at him, her face the most serious he had seen in a long time.

"It is the magic of the Mighty Ones, the ancestors of all faeries. They were the judges of evil, held in high regard. I believe it is the magical binding of a person, in this case, Rhetoric."

Enol listened to her intently as she spoke. "Is this dangerous for Madrena?"

Ciera stared once more in his eyes and said, "Only if she gets in the way."

He took her hand, squeezing it, and together they walked into the darkness of the hallway, ready for whatever it held.

* * *

His fortress was falling down around him and his plan to control the books as well...and Rhetoric knew this. He stood at the top of the tallest turret, the only one that was not burning, having left Ciera when the elk he had enslaved ran through the room. Without the elk to push the sun wheel, the mist he had discovered years before, was useless.

He looked down at the mist still slowly moving on his arms and across his chest. It would not be long and it would stop moving altogether. It had no power of movement on its own but with the elk pumping it, moving it, and the spell he had on it, he had been able to use it, concealing his fortress, controlling his enemies like IBNot and Anhur to do his bidding. He had to think.

Rhetoric looked down over the turret wall. The courtyard was littered with the bodies of his soldiers, the ravens and the gate of his fortress was smashed outward from the stampeding elk. He saw the fairies and elk as they made their way back across the rock wall to the meadows on the other side.

Looking up he cursed the blue sky and thought of the books as he glanced over to the turret that had held captive the faeries that had appeared with those books. Fire spewed from it. His ravens had searched Whisper Hollow thoroughly they said, questioning and killing all who there. There had been no trunk, no thirteenth book, only the crown with thirteen emeralds. It could be with Enol but he did not think so. IBNot had searched their camp as they slept and as they fought the ravens. No trunk, no book.

Enol had only just been able to enter the fortress. Something or someone had been able to break the chain of mist that had held Ciera, the faeries, and Quinn. Only the power of the thirteenth book would have the ability to break the spell he had over it; and how had Ciera managed to get into the fortress without his knowing.

Rhetoric raised his face to the now blue skies above roaring, "Aaaahhhh!" as he remembered the first chain of mist that had nearly knocked him from his chair, and the only person in the room with the person who had been held by it… Madrena. It must be she that is in control of the thirteenth book! She, that has it! She, that he must kill!

Angrily Rhetoric pulled open the door to the upper floor of the turret and ran down the stairs he had climbed slowly earlier in thought. Maybe all was not lost.

* * *

Madrena and Adren had watched as Fire and Quinn disappeared down the hallway, his red eyes able to light the way until the two of them could be seen no more. Anya watched from behind the wheel and it was then that she saw her chance. Silently standing she picked up a stone from the floor, hitting Adren from behind. Madrena turned as he fell to the floor unconscious, pulling her sword as she did.

"You've grown up my dear. How well has momma taught you to use that sword?" said Anya snidely, pulling hers as well.

Madrena glanced quickly down at Adren, his head was bleeding but he was breathing then back up at Anya noticing the crown. Her eyes sparkled and she held her sword high and to the right. "Let's just say you may have hit the wrong person in the head."

Anya spread her wings revealing the notches preventing flight and Madrena responded in turn, spreading hers.

"Couldn't imagine not being able to fly Auntie," she said sarcastically, smiling and adding, "How's that working for you?" as she flew up, then down towards her, sword slashing.

Her aunt responded by swinging upwards with all her might, their swords connecting so perfectly that Madrena felt the strength of her and was sent flying over the wheel to the stone floor below.

Anya wasted no time running around it and stood above her saying, "When one ability leaves, another ability becomes stronger my dear. It works just fine."

The blade of the sword came down quickly and Madrena rolled, avoiding it, coming to her feet. She swung out defiantly and once again their swords met in the middle, but this time

Madrena held her own and Anya's eyes widened as she felt her strength.

"Tell me where the thirteenth book is and I will let you live," she grunted.

The faerie princess responded by pulling her sword free and lashing out repeatedly driving back her aunt against the stone wall, pinning her.

"Sometimes my dear aunt, the answer can be staring you right in the face!" she said it forcefully, their eyes glaring at each other briefly until Anya's glanced away.

From behind Madrena heard her father's voice, "Stand down, Anya!" and without thinking she looked back quickly seeing her mother kneel down and check Adren as her aunt responded with, "Never!" Letting go of her sword with one hand, Anya pulled her dagger from its sheath, pushing it deep into Madrena. Enol ran at them both as his daughter slumped to the floor. He saw her fingers barely slide through the triscale of the crown, pulling it free as he swung his sword angrily toward Anya.

Adren's voice could be heard from behind as his wife's evil sister's sword and his met in mid air. "No!" he screamed seeing Madrena lying on the stone across the room. He rose, running to her side with Ciera as Enol battled Anya around to the other side of the wheel. Madrena's eyes were open and she gazed up as Adren propped her in his arms, her fingers still clutching the crown.

"Focus, my darling," he said gently. "You are the book, the book is you. Take us back to the cave. Not just to it, but back, understand?"

Ciera placed a hand on his shoulder understanding fully. "Yes Madrena, concentrate. You must go back to the page of your time in the cave with Adren, back to the beginning."

All the while Enol and Anya fought, blow after blow. Anya

with her sword in one hand and her dagger in the other, Madrena's blood still on its tip, fended off Enol's every swing. She was strong, very strong and she heard what was said to Madrena.

Anya lunged forward, pushing Enol backwards step by step till she caught his sword, flinging it across the room. The clanging noise of it against the wall caused Ciera and Adren to look up from Madrena at the two, watching as Enol jumped and rolled over the top of one of the spokes placing it between them.

Immediately Ciera stood, removing the dragonfly dagger from her sheath, tossing it to her husband, saying to Madrena, "Go now! Back to the cave!" as she drew her sword and went to her husband aid. Her daughter gave her a slow wink she never saw and both her and Adren disappeared, never seeing Enol slump to the floor as Anya's dagger once again met its mark.

* * *

In the moment it took for them to arrive in the cave a tear ran down Adren's cheek. Somehow this woman, this faerie princess, this woman he loved with all his heart must not die. Madrena's eyes opened just barely, her lips moving, no sound coming from them until a whisper came through. "The book, get our book." Adren stood, turning, scanning the cave and finding the book exactly where she had left it on the trunk next to the puddle created by the water that ran down the wall in a steady trickle. It lay there open and as he picked it up he glanced at the page of Quiviera. It seemed so long ago.

"Should I close it my love?" he asked. Madrena laid there quiet, her chest barely moving, blood still soaking her clothes. Something was not right. He had been sure that this would work.

Then her eyes opened once more and a whisper came, "Yes."

Carefully he set the book on her chest, placing each arm across it and then he knew. He looked up and around the cave then back at Madrena whose face was now terribly pale and put his arms around her remembering that she had summoned the book to Quiviera. "We are not really back yet are we?"

A whisper, "No, hold on" could barely be heard…and the pages of the book glowed between its closed covers, the triscale on its cover shining brightest of all.

Adren watched fascinated at the power of Madrena and her book, their book as she called it. Large transparent pages with just the outline of objects on them, visibly seemed to turn in front of him. At first they seemed to turn quickly. There was a flash of the inner courtyard, Anya, Ciera, and Enol and the wheel; of turret rooms burning; the camp at the two rivers flashed by; and then they were flying, with Madrena below him. Now Quiviera and Quinn, healthy and transparent and then the pages seemed to slow and he could feel her heartbeat. It was slowing too.

Adren could see the meadow with Logren and the other elk before him but somehow see Quiviera on the next page as well. "You must hold on Madrena!" he yelled shaking her. He must keep her alive! "Just two more pages my love," and the page flipped and they were back in the meadow in Quiviera where they had first met Quinn. He squeezed her tightly kissing her cheek. "One more, just one more my love." …and suddenly they were there, back in the cave, the glow of the triscale and the pages slowly fading.

Adren looked around quickly. Yes, this is as it was then. He felt it. They were there. She had successfully brought them back.

"I told you to hold on," came a whisper.

"I will never let go," he said now looking down at Madrena as another tear traced down his cheek and she wiped it away saying, "Nor I."

He touched her chin, color was coming back to her face and her eyes seemed more open and brighter than moments before. Still holding her in one arm, he moved the book. The bleeding had stopped.

"How do you feel?" he asked.

She moved her hand across the place where Anya's dagger had nearly taken her life.

"I feel nothing."

Her eyes filled with wonder and awe, as she looked over at their book, fully aware that they would not be here without its help. While she had to work through its pages to get to the meadow, and the turret rooms to free her mother and the other fairies, it had worked through her to save her life. It must be hidden well she thought. There was so much more to learn about it.

Madrena's hand once again felt the place where her wound had been and she remembered Rhetoric, Anya and where they needed to be. Placing her hands on Adren's shoulders she stood slowly with his help, realizing she felt no pain at all, unable to stop staring at her blood soaked stomach…amazing.

Gently Adren took the crown from her fingers that were still laced in the triscale. He moved the stray hairs from her face placing it on her head and for one instant he was sure that he had seen the triscale glow. It had never glowed while on Anya's head. It knew it was home.

"How do I look?" she asked, looking up at him.

He gazed at the crown then her eyes. They were once again their sparkling self.

He smiled, relieved, "Incredible as always," and he kissed her softly. "Are you ready?" The corners of her mouth curled up, "Yes, except for this terrible stain on my outfit, I am."

Adren chuckled and she continued. "We have one stop to make before we return to the fortress."

"And where would that be?" he asked.

"Reliving the past has its advantages. It makes you see things you should have done, and gives you the chance to do them."

Madrena slid her hand into his, winked and instantly they were in Quiviera with her grandfather, forward just three pages and Quinn was telling her not to forget what he had left for her in his room…Rhetoric's book.

* * *

Enol lay there bleeding and unconscious, having hit his head on a spoke when falling, but not dead. Anya's dagger had only gone in about two inches before Ciera had charged, catching her off guard and she had released her hold on it to fend off the blows of her sister's sword. Anya then jumped on the rim of the wheel running to the other side of it, leaving Ciera at Enol's side.

The Queen of the Faeries knelt, quickly pulling the dagger from her husband's chest, thankful that it was not the dragonfly dagger and tossed it to the far end of the room.

Her sister scowled, "That makes two for him now, doesn't it? One more with the right dagger and the books and their power will be ours."

Ciera glared at her sister still squatting at her husband's side. She brushed the hair from his eyes and noticed the dragonfly dagger still clasp in his right hand. There was blood halfway up it. It would be useless against Rhetoric. Her mind flashed to Adren then back to the dagger in her husband's hand then to Anya. She had been wounded too. Their eyes met.

"The books will not ever be yours Anya…not ever." She

said it matter of fact as she scanned her sister's body for the wound, and found it. The black striped woman that used to be the sister she played with as a child gritted her teeth, shooting back, "I should kill both of you now. I heard what was said. Madrena is the one we want. She is the one in control of the thirteenth book."

Ciera stood slowly, turning fully towards her, wings tight against her back. Easily she stepped up on the wheel hub that had once encircled the evil mist but now held only a seemingly bottomless pit. She could see now that Anya's wound was bleeding more than her husband's. This was not the sister she had played with as a child.

"That sounded like an invitation sister," Ciera said, moving her fingers saying 'come on' with them. She watched intently as her sister side stepped the wall, never showing pain from her wound. She was indeed a warrior.

Ciera continued mocking her. "What was it Day said you told Smoke before you injured him…oh yes. We are done here." Nimbly she stepped backwards out onto the spoke behind her, jumping to the next one at the same time causing Anya to have to turn sharply, her face grimacing ever so slightly now with pain.

"I see my husband hit his mark as well, sister."

"It is nothing!" Anya's sword came around swiftly showing the strength she still possessed. Their swords met three times. Ciera pushed at her the third time, jumping to the next spoke away from Enol. Once again her sister winched as she turned to face her, and Ciera smiled. "I think you're fibbing," she taunted.

Anya swung out somewhat wildly, slicing through air as Ciera once again jumped to the next yoke, each time placing her sister with her back to the pit in the center of the wheel hub. The stain on her shirt was becoming larger yet, her breathing more and more labored. The spokes themselves were only three inches wide, but Ciera balanced easily upon them, fending off her every advance, jumping between them over and over again as Anya struggled to side step, keep her balance and handle the pain that was now becoming overwhelming. She was tiring and they both knew it, as she continued to struggle to get her breath.

"You are strong, my sister," said Ciera, "It is a shame you chose evil. Don't you know it never wins?"

Her answer was forced through her labored breathing, "But it is never forgotten," and she swung out, this time feeling the pain of the wound worse than ever as her and Ciera's swords met. She cringed as their swords clanged together, holding her elbow tightly to her wound and fell backwards into the pit.

Ciera stepped onto the wall, crouching, peering down. "I will remember you, my sister…not as what you became, but for what you once were."

She gazed downwards just for a moment then her eyes went from the pit to the spot where Madrena and Adren had been. She must believe.

"Never did like her much," rasped out a voice from behind her causing her head to jerk around. It was Rhetoric, his book under his arm. His words were dry now, not gurgled here and there as before. The mist within him had dried up. She stood slowly, turning towards him…the pit, now at her own back. Ciera side stepped to the left of the spoke in front of her, jumping down to the stone floor of the room, her sword held high.

"You will not win this fight, Rhetoric. Give up, and I will let you live."

A loud evil laugh came from him, from somewhere deep inside, the kind of laugh that bad dreams are made of. Ciera glanced quickly back at the dagger in her husbands hand. The laughing stopped abruptly. He had seen her look over at it. "That dagger is of no use to you. I will tell you once more Ciera that I am not afraid of you. It is you that will die and then your husband will taste my own dragonfly dagger," he snarled at her, patting the dagger at his side. Ciera glanced at his side, remembering the gleam of metal she had seen earlier. Remembering what Adren had said about if there was two, there could be more. Rhetoric tossed his book to the side sending it sliding across the stone floor bumping the wall with a thud and he pulled his sword and Ciera's eyebrows rose as the third dragonfly dagger came into view. Adren had been right!

Without a second thought she lunged at him wielding the sword in a criss cross pattern, so he could not strike before she could. Rhetoric did not wait for her to reach him. He charged as well. A full head taller than she, he swung his sword down upon her repeatedly. Pushing her back till their swords interlocked and with his strength shoved hard, sending her across the room, sliding on the jagged stone.

He wasted no time moving towards Enol as he dropped his sword and pulled the dagger from its sheath. Ciera pulled herself up, standing but unsteady, bruised and bloodied from the stone.

Then suddenly Madrena's voice could be heard causing Rhetoric to twirl around and her own head to spin toward it. "You cannot and will not win Rhetoric," she said simply.

The black striped man glared at her, momentarily forgetting about Enol, a thousand thoughts racing through his mind, when a slap on the wood of the sun wheel grabbed all their attentions.

"She and the book are one!" grunted Anya as she pulled herself from the depths of pit and stood, winching in pain, still clutching her wound with her elbow, barely able to maintain her balance.

Rhetoric returned his glare to Madrena, the crown on her head and those green eyes. His mind raced again thinking of this, as he sized up the man at her side. No sword showed over his shoulder. His only weapon was a dagger at his side. Dropping his own dragonfly dagger back into its sheath, he bent down, snatching up his sword from the stone floor and came up at a run toward the both of them. Quickly Adren pulled Madrena's sword from her back, lunging toward him and their swords met. Rhetoric knew at once that he had met his match.

Picking up Rhetoric's book, Madrena raced across the room, shoving the barely conscious Anya easily back into the pit. "Don't worry dear auntie, company's a'comin!"

Her aunt descended down with wide eyes staring straight back up at Madrena and she screamed, "I will be back! I will finish the page!"

The faerie princess stared down till no sign of her could be seen. "And I will be waiting."

She turned to her father. Her mother had made her way to him and was helping him to a sitting position. Across the room Rhetoric and Adren were exchanging many blows. Rhetoric grunted with his swings trying to make them more powerful while Adren hit him with a fist in the face every chance he could. Yes, he was the better warrior. His parents had taught him well.

Madrena turned to her mother, yelling over the clang of the swords. "Take him out of here!"

"No, we will not leave you and Adren!" came back her mother as her father struggled to his feet. "The book of Rhetoric…"

Madrena glanced over at Rhetoric and Adren then back at her, cutting in, not letting her finish. "I know, now please go! Take him out!"

Ciera gave her the worried mother look but knew her

daughter was right. Her husband, her father was a sure target in his present condition for the dragonfly dagger that still hung on Rhetoric's waist. "We will wait outside!" she yelled.

Madrena nodded, turning her attention to Adren as Ciera all but carried Enol out of the courtyard and down the hall to safety. The faerie princess jumped up on the sun wheel's hub, side stepping as Anya had around the rim to the far side.

"Over here Adren, you must bring him closer!"

The dragonfly faerie heard her and pushed hard trying to drive him back towards the wheel, but Rhetoric heard too and swung his sword even harder, driving Adren down to his knees at one point, causing him to have to roll on the stone to avoid the sharp edge of the blade as it swooshed by.

Madrena watched breathlessly as they fought, only the sudden warmth of the book she held stopped her. Slowly she looked down at the book. The previous title 'The Book of Rhetoric' faded and a shape formed on the cover. It was a triscale like the one on her crown. They were one and the same and they were both glowing. Opening the cover, she scanned the words inside as the pages of the book began to glow illuminating the ink on the page. She began reading the words inside aloud, holding the book over the pit.

Rhetoric!

We the Brehon…theJudges of Old

Condemn you for the evil you have done!

In the Name of the Mighty Ones and The Old Ones!

We ground you to the Depths of the Wheel

and seal you within it!

By the Power of the Triscale

You are commanded to enter!

Madrena looked briefly up from the book after finishing the

last line. Adren was barely holding his own, and their movement toward the wheel was slow. Rhetoric was fighting like never before. With no mist now moving upon him, and no magic to draw on, he fought for his life; and now the words Madrena read seemed to pound within his head, giving him the feeling of someone pulling from behind, pulling him towards the pit. Between Adren's powerful blows with his sword and the strength Rhetoric had to exert just to fend them off, and the pulling, he felt himself tiring…fast.

Over and over again Madrena read the passage of her ancestors that beckoned Rhetoric into the pit, till finally he was within range of its grasp. Unseen hands seemed to tug at him from behind and the advances of Adren were pushing him into them, forcing him to wedge himself between the spokes of the sun wheel and its hub.

A light came from above him, and he glanced up as their swords met once more. The glow of the triscale from the book and Madrena's crown reflected off the sunlight shining down from the skies above. It blinded him, burning his eyes, and he covered them with his arms briefly without thought of Adren and the sword he held. Rhetoric swung his sword one last time, eyes barely open, still blinded by the light of the triscale. Their swords locked together at the hilt and Adren, without a second thought, pushed hard, flipping him over the rim and into the pit.

Madrena, still reading the ligature, did not see his hand as it grabbed out catching the loose end of her wrap pulling her in with him. Adren dove forward, waist balanced on the rim, one leg hooked under a spoke, catching the book and her hand as she tumbled in.

"Hold on!" he yelled down at her. Her eyes were wide. Her voice rasped out words that he could not understand. Then he saw the redness and blue coming to her face. One side of her wrap had been tied into her belt that held her dagger and its sheath so they could be readily accessed and the other had been free…the one Rhetoric had grabbed. She was choking.

Madrena pulled at the wrap that was tightening against her throat, almost clawing at it. She knew that in a moment or two she would lose consciousness. She would be dead weight and with Rhetoric below her Adren would not be able to hold them.

Rhetoric pulled on the wrap trying to get a good grip on it so as to climb up, unaware of Madrena's choking predicament.

Adren yelled down to her, "Your dagger, can you reach it? You must cut it! Cut the wrap!"

Her eyes were wide, she was having trouble focusing, but she had heard and reached down, her fingertips just touching it. Her eyes drove into Adren. The love of his life was dying and he could do nothing. He had tried to pull both of them up but the weight was too great. Her eyes blinked, she was fading.

"Madrena! Stay with me!" It was then that he noticed Rhetoric. He had given up on climbing her wrap and was pulling the dragonfly dagger from its sheath with his free hand.

"If I am to die today, then I will take you with me little one!"

His hand went back as Adren felt his own dragonfly dagger slide from Tarin's sheath. He turned to find Ciera tossing it into the air, catching it by the tip, and slinging it at Rhetoric before he could release his. The dagger met its mark burying itself to the hilt deep in his chest. He grabbed at it, without thought, with the hand that had gripped the wrap and fell with his own dragonfly dagger still in his hand into the depths of the pit.

Madrena was limp and together they pulled her up, laying

her gently on the stone floor and loosening the wrap. Adren placed his hand on her face, tracing the line of her chin.

"Do not leave me now, sweetie…"

Tears formed in both their eyes as Ciera said, "Wake up my little princess, it is not time for you. Wake up."

Madrena coughed, and they both breathed in at the same time in relief. Slowly she opened her eyes, her voice just a whisper for the second time that day.

"Rhetoric?"

Adren smiled down at her. "Your mother, it was she." He looked from Madrena to Ciera then back again to Madrena. "Please remind me never to get in a contest with her where daggers are concerned!"

Their faerie princess smiled but it faded quickly, "The book…did it?"

"No," answered Adren, turning and picking it up. "It is here."

"Help me up please. The pit, it must be sealed."

"I don't think either one of them are coming back up any time soon," he said nodding toward it.

Madrena smiled at him and glanced over to her mother, giving her a wink as Adren helped her to her feet. "True magic never dies," she said simply, stepping up on the side of the wheel.

Once again the triscale was glowing on the book, beckoning her to open it and she did. There was one more ligature to read, one more to seal Rhetoric's and Anya's fate forever. Together both the triscale on her crown and the book glowed even brighter than before as she read.

Rhetoric!
We the Brehon…the Judges of Old
Condemn you for the evil you have done!

In the Name of the Mighty Ones and The Old Ones!
We ground you to the Depths of the Wheel
and seal you within it!
By the Power of the Triscale
Your Baneful hold upon this land
Is ended!

Madrena read the ligature twice and during the second the book floated up from her hands, the cover closing, the triscale still glowing, and the shape of the entire book changed. They watched as it grew to fit the entrance to the pit, rounding itself and settling on top of it. There was a snap and a fire started on the far side quickly moving in opposite directions along the edge of the book and the sun wheel toward them, spewing flames and burning embers to the sides…sealing it completely. All three stood silent.

*　*　*

Enol sat outside leaning against the fortress. His chest hurt…a lot, but his eyes never left the smashed gate. He grew impatient and called over to Logren. The great elk bent his head forward stretching down to hear him as he half whispered.

"Do you think you can fit through the gate?"

Logren looked him straight in the eyes, "I will go as far as I can, then I will go further. I will not return without them."

He smiled and Enol smiled back. They had become friends for life and they both knew it. The great elk turned charging through the gate.

Stones from the top of the arch fell as his huge mass squeezed under it and into the outer courtyard. Seeing the tracks of his son and the other elk created as they headed toward the gate, he followed them back to the hallway and peered down it. There was only darkness and it was much too small for his enormous size. Attempting to fit might bring down the entire fortress on everyone.

"Ciera!" he bellowed. There was no answer and he called her name once more. This time an answer!

"Yes Logren, we are here!" They had been mesmerized by the book and its powers, amazed at the power between its covers until Cedrick shrieked from high above the inner courtyard and Ciera had signaled him all was well, and then they had heard Logren.

They came around the turn in the hallway and the great elk smiled as they walked into the light. His eyes quickly filled with concern when he saw the blood on Madrena's outfit. She had seen his stare and spread her arms as far as she could around him.

"No need for concern, my friend." She patted her stomach showing there was no wound.

Ciera was already outside and in her husband's arms as Adren, Logren and Madrena came through the gate. There were hugs and kisses between mother, father and daughter, and a handshake between Enol and Adren that showed respect and admiration.

Ciera turned to Logren. "Your son, was he with the other elk?" she asked softly.

His face beamed with pride as he answered, "He was the one who carried your friend Smoke. Thank you all."

Two other elk stood close to the stone wall and they stomped their hooves in agreement.

Madrena noticed Cinq, Saynk, and Sunck flying towards them, waving and she waved back, but Adren caught her arm. "They are not waving, they are pointing!"

All heads turned to see the captain of the ravens diving down at them from above, talons out. Adren jumped in the air, flying up fast to intercept, but the raven anticipated this, shoving him aside hard with his head, hitting him full force in the stomach, sending him plummeting into the Zacarra. There was no hesitation. The raven increased his speed, thoroughly focused on his target...Enol. He never saw the talons of Cedrick and Karnan as they came swooping in together. They took him by the wings up far up into the sky, and tore him to shreds.

Cinq, Saynk and Sunck wasted no time diving into the rough waters, bringing Adren to the clearing at their feet.

Madrena moved his chin gently. "No you don't! You cannot be rid of me that easily!" She said it forcefully, shaking him by the shoulders.

His eyes opened slowly and he spoke. "Nor would I want to."

A screech from above caused them all to look up once more. Cedrick and Karnan were circling and Ciera answered the great birds. "Yes, my friends, we will leave now."

She turned to her husband, "Let's get you up," adding, "Adren are you able to walk?" The dragonfly faerie was just coming to a standing position with the help of Madrena. With a small blush spreading across his cheeks he answered, "Yes, nothing hurt here but my pride."

Everyone smiled and the moment of comradery was broken only by Enol asking Ciera, "Did you say the fortress walls were impregnated with the mist and that they were weaker for it?" Ciera nodded, but before she could continue Logren spoke up, having heard him. "The inner walls are now engulfed in flames. A few hits from the three of us," he nodded towards the other elk, "And you can consider this fortress a memory."

Enol nodded at the the massive elk as Saynk and Sunck came to his sides, placing his arms over their shoulders. "We will see you on the other side then," the two water fairies warbled together to Logren, and up they flew followed by

Madrena, Adren and Cinq.

Ciera stepped forward touching the great elk's face, "Have fun with that," she said nodding towards the fortress.

"Oh, we will," he answered, having something to smile about for the first time in a while.

Ciera flew up, watching while the elk started pounding the walls repeatedly, burying Rhetoric, Anya, and the key of their ancestors forever…

One Year Later...

THE OLD man sat outside the home of Enol and Ciera, his beloved Quiviera out of the clouds, once again grounded as it should be and always had been. He watched as the faeries of Whisper Hollow, Adren and his granddaughter gathered wood for the fire they would have that night. It was he that would tell the story...a story of times to come. Madrena stood and waved from the meadow, holding flowers in the air she had found, for him to see. His thoughts however, were not of flowers as he waved back, but of the page on which his granddaughter most assuredly would have died if it had been finished. He had since buried that page deep within her book, so deep that no one could ever do just that...but who knows? For as we all know now, anything is possible between the covers of a book, if you believe.

CPSIA information can be obtained at www.ICGtesting.com
Printed in the USA
BVOW021552201112

306051BV00001B/2/P

9 781609 766290